Joker in the Deck

Richard S. Prather

AN [e-reads]BOOK
New York, NY

Copyright © 1964 by Richard S. Prather
Copyright renewed 1992 by Richard S. Prather
First e-reads publication 2002
www.e-reads.com
ISBN 0-7592-2622-9

For
ART and ARLY JACOBS

Table of Contents

One

The more some things change, as the saying goes, the more they stay the same. For example — just for fun — take sex.

Here I was, standing near the swimming pool clutching a bourbon-and-water highball, and over by the snack bar were Adam and Eve.

This Eve was a long-legged, voluptuous-looking, slinky, busty, hippy bomb, an Adam bomb, and the very male male was Adam Preston, and this was the twentieth century — so it was the twentieth century: he still looked like a man gnashing fig leaves and it was eight to five she was giving him that old Garden-of-Eden applesauce. The way they were carrying on you just *knew* those original sinners must have had a pretty good idea in the first place. At least, I'd say so.

But I'd say so anyway; I'm Shell Scott.

I'm a private detective, but for a change I wasn't detecting much of anything, except what was going on over by the snack bar, which even a blind non-detective couldn't very easily have missed. Instead, on this balmy Saturday night, the fifteenth of June, I was sixty miles from *Sheldon Scott, Investigations* — my one-man office in downtown Los Angeles — enjoying myself in Laguna Beach at the newest and jazziest land development on the explosively booming Southern California coast: 1500 acres stretching from the sea up into the low Laguna hills, complete with paved roads, underground utilities, an eighteen-hole golf course, subdivisions containing hundreds of king-size lots, and two dozen model homes ready and waiting for anybody with lots of money.

The whole thing was the joint project and promotion of the afore-mentioned Adam Preston, and my long-time friend, drinking partner, and lively companion, Jim Paradise. Since Jim, who had invited me

1

down here tonight, was the prime mover and major investor in the project, it was called, appropriately enough, Laguna Paradise.

Jim and I were standing among fifty people or so on the cement deck of a blue-lighted swimming pool before one of the luxurious model homes, and three or four hundred more citizens were milling about on the grounds nearby. Two hundred yards west was the ocean, and midway between the crashing surf and the spot where Jim and I stood was the main sales office of Laguna Paradise.

Atop the office was a large plastic map of the entire development, illuminated from inside, and whenever a home or lot was sold the corresponding section of the map lighted up brilliantly — while at the same time head salesman Wally West cried joyously over a public address system that "Lot number sixteen has just been sold to DANIEL GRAYMOUNT, the *well-known movie producer*," or named whoever had made the purchase, repeating the person's name loudly numerous times, much to the delight of said person, who sometimes became so delighted he went back to buy another lot.

Both before and after such exciting comments a five-piece combo played everything from Dixieland to the Twist and its successor, the Grump, which is a combination of bumps and grinds and almost total capitulation. Down on Coast Boulevard three arc lights swept the sky, telling everybody for miles around that something jazzy was going on in the Laguna area.

In addition to all that razzle-dazzle, Jim Paradise and Adam Preston had employed, cleverly I thought, a half-dozen models from Hollywood's top emporium of feminine pulchritude, Alexandria's. These six — one of whom was Eve, tall, busty Eve Angers — suitably briefed and clad in suitably brief outfits, were available to answer the questions of potential customers. Since the outfits were high-heeled shoes, net "showgirl" hose, snug white shorts and fuzzy white sweaters, a lot of people asked questions, and a couple of guys even got their faces slapped.

A minute ago Jim had left to get us a couple more bourbon-and-waters. Now he headed back from the bar, nodding to people, waving, flashing his quick grin at others. Jim Paradise was so crammed with energy and male hormones and vital juices you half expected him to glow in the dark, a tall handsome man who looked half pirate and half Apollo. Several people watched him as he walked back, and there had

2

been some eyeballing from the citizens earlier when Jim and I had been standing together. Probably because we're both pretty big, but also because of the contrast between us.

I'm six-two and weigh two hundred and six pounds after three bourbon highballs — which I'd just had — and Jim was twenty pounds lighter but an inch taller. My short-cropped hair is as white as the angle-iron brows which shoot up and out over my gray eyes and then slant sharply down like the contrails of pooped rockets, while Jim's hair was coal black and his eyes were the blue-green of deep water.

Both of us got a lot of sun, but Jim was even more bronzed than I. He looked like a tall, civilized devil, burned brown by those flames down where they toast people. There was even a kind of satanic cast to his features, the dark eyes bold, nose straight and a little sharp, a mouth I'd heard women describe as "reckless," and a go-to-hell grin.

He handed me my drink, gulped a slug of his own and said cheerfully, "Shell, this sure as hell looks like success. What does a guy do with a million dollars?"

"Why, he saves it," I said. "What else?"

He scowled. "I never thought of that."

"You wouldn't want to spend it on riotous living — "

"I wouldn't?"

"Wine, women and song — "

"The *hell* I — "

" — or such foolishness." I grinned. "After all, a million saved is a million earned."

Jim nodded vigorously. "That makes no sense at all. By God, you're right! I'll save it!"

"And live a sane, sober life."

"A sober life," he said solemnly. "I'll drink to that." He had another belt of his bourbon and went on dully, "Here's to sobriety, piety, chastity, insanity, stupidity — "

I didn't hear the rest of whatever he was drinking to. I wasn't listening. I was looking — at something which would cure diplopia at thirty paces, at a woman who had just come to the top of steps which led up here from a landscaped patio below, a woman who was now walking toward Jim and me. She was wearing the Alexandria's outfit, obviously one of the models, and obviously one of the two or three I hadn't met. But I was *going* to meet her, if I had to walk barefoot through snapping crocodiles.

"Jim," I said, "who is she? Some pal — why didn't you tell me? Who — "

Ignoring my question he said sadly, "And so we drink to chastity. Yes, we'll have a chastity belt; then a snort to — "

"The hell with that noise. I've given up all that. Jim, dammit, who is she?"

A quick rough guess at those smooth curves, the color and sizzling impact, would have been: About five feet, five inches tall; an incredible 37-22-36 that was much more than the sum of its parts; a puff of blonde hair, impish red lips, sparkling eyes — evolution's end, no matter which end you were looking at.

"You refer, I presume, to Laurie," Jim said.

"Laurie? Ah...." It was the face of a wise warm angel, plus a body that was the ultimate in feminine voluptuousness, a combination to turn idle glances into double-takes and double-takes into stares.

"Laurie Lee," Jim went on. "I guess you noticed she's a girl. I guess you want to meet her." Without waiting for my answer he called, "Laurie!"

She stopped, turned her head, smiled and stepped toward us. "Hi, Jim," she said. "Going great tonight, isn't it?"

Up close she was even better. She glanced at me from light honey-brown eyes, then looked back at Jim, but that quick glance went into me like a knife into soup. It was a face to stop a heart, a body to make vegetarians eat meatballs.

"Hello!" I said. "Hello there. How do you do? I'm delighted — "

"I haven't introduced you yet," Jim interrupted. Then he bowed slightly and said, "Laurie, this ape is Sheldon Scott. Shell, Laurie Lee. He's a private detective, and you should stay away — "

"What do you mean, ape?" I said. "You selfish — "

"How do you do, Sheldon?" Laurie said, and smiled. The voice was sweet and warm and the glance she gave me could have roasted weenies.

"Hot dog!" I said. "I mean, that's not what I meant. My mind was, uh — call me Shell, please. Nobody calls me Sheldon. Not even my enemies."

"I'll bet," she said, as if she didn't, "you've got simply ferocious enemies."

"Don't kid yourself," Jim broke in again. "That's what happened to his face. The broken nose, that fine scar over his eye, the small piece missing from his left ear, that's how ferocious. Well, now 'that you've seen the havoc wrought by saps, brass knuckles, husbands, turn your pretty head away — "

But Laurie had stepped close to me, was leaning even closer. "Why, you *do*," she said. "You do have a bit gone from your ear." She sounded delighted.

"If it will make you any happier I'll snatch the rest of it off, like Gauguin — "

"Van Gogh," said Jim.

" — like that nut," I continued. She was very close, looking up at me, breath warm on my cheek.

"How did it happen?" she asked, then suddenly said, "But that's none of my business, is it?"

"Of course it is," I said, friendly as could be. "Anything, everything — "

"Then how *did* it happen?"

"Oh, that. A little gunman took a shot at me and missed — almost missed, that is. He nipped my ear."

She laughed merrily. "Oh, you men! You're worse than Jim."

I'm not exactly the haughty headwaiter type, and probably she thought I'd caught my ear in some gears while working in the corner gas station. The funny thing was that a little hood did shoot it off. And it was the last ear he ever shot off.

Right then a strange thing happened. At least it was strange that I should see the guy when I was casually thinking about guns and gunmen. I'd turned my head the other way for some reason — actually, if you want to know, so Laurie could see my good ear — and a not unfamiliar face came into view.

It was a thin face, on a short, thin guy who was standing about where Eve had been earlier. He was leaning against the snack bar, talking to Adam Preston and stuffing bite-size sandwiches into his mouth. I couldn't remember where it had been, but I knew I'd seen him before.

And a nerve in my noodle wiggled: Trouble.

Two

This guy had the mobster look, anyway. Dark blue suit, expensive, but a little more extreme than was currently fashionable, cut a bit wide in the shoulders, snug in the middle. Pointed black shoes polished to a high gloss. A black snap-brim hat on his head. He turned, glanced this way, and I saw the pinched features, the coldly uncommunicative eyes. Trouble, all right, some kind of trouble. But I couldn't make him, and it bothered me.

Laurie was saying something. I turned toward her.

"Got to run," she said. "If I goof any more, the boss might fire me."

"Fat chance," said Jim.

As she started off I said, "Laurie, since quitting time is ten, maybe we could continue the conversation then. I'll tell you about the time the Mafia stuck me in cement and dropped me in the ocean."

"Did they really do that?"

"Not really, but it's a whale of a story."

"Well . . ."

Jim said, "Why not? Maybe we could make it a foursome." Laurie seemed agreeable to the idea and he continued, "In Hollywood, maybe? You girls all live there, don't you?"

Laurie nodded, and said she lived at the Claymore, which was only a block from Alexandria's. Jim asked, "Any of the other girls live there?"

"Only Judith. Oh, Eve too, now — she joined the agency a day or two before we were sent out on this job and asked me if I knew a nice place to stay. I told her about the Claymore, so she moved in there, too. The other three girls," she added with a smile, "live with their husbands."

Jim winced, and said he'd seen Eve go into the model home behind us a few minutes before. He left and soon returned with her.

6

He was, apparently, still trying to convince her, and she, apparently, remained unconvinced.

"It sounds fun," Eve said. "I can't, though. Really. I've got to . . ." She paused for a few seconds, thinking, then said, "But maybe — can I tell you for sure in half an hour or so? There's something I have to, well, check on."

Probably, I thought, it was two or three other guys who'd asked her for dates. For nights in L. A. Or weekends in Bermuda. Or simply no telling. Because there was a lot of this Eve Angers and not a bit too much.

Laurie was maybe five feet, five inches tall and marvelously proportioned, but she looked almost diminutive next to Eve, a tall lass of five-nine or so, a big woman with soft, flowing curves, long lovely legs, and a superbly abundant bosom actually astonishing in the fuzzy white sweater.

Laurie was tanned, active, energetic, while Eve's skin was smooth and pale and she moved with a slow grace, deliberately, languorously. Eve's eyes were the pale green of a Burmese cat's, slanted, oriental, dangerous-looking eyes, and her hair was thick, loosely waved, a glossy black, with little-girl bangs in feathery arcs inky against the white of her forehead. The bangs seemed out of place on Eve, because there was nothing else little-girl about her. Her eyes and brows were heavily made up, and orange-red lipstick outlined her wide, sullen mouth. Salmon-colored polish glittered on her long fingernails. Except for the black hair she seemed a woman of pastels — pale eyes and mouth and nails and smooth white skin — but hot pastels.

Jim told Eve that was fine, but to let us know as soon as she could because the suspense was killing him. She nodded, smiled, and began slinking away. We watched the long lovely legs depart, hips swaying seductively above them, and it was a stimulating vista. Laurie said she'd check with us later, and followed Eve, and watching Laurie was even more stimulating.

I said to Jim, "Who's the cat talking to Adam?"

He looked, shook his head. "Nobody I ever saw before. Why?"

"Just curious. I've seen him somewhere."

Jim hied himself to the bar for more bourbon. I walked to the snack bar, loaded some of the little sandwiches, and hunks of cheese, turkey, lobster, onto a paper plate.

The little man was saying something about "Brea," I thought, and then he added, "You better change your mind, pally — tonight. Matter of fact, it's got to be tonight."

Adam laughed, as if vastly amused. "You give me a pain in the coccyx, my dear fellow. There's really nothing further to discuss — "

"Don't give me that high-toned lip. You ain't dealing with no little old ladies from Pasadena. And this is goddamn important to my people — "

"The hell with your people." Adam's voice had changed, lost its light bantering tone, gotten lower and harder. "And the hell with you. They know my terms. They can take it or shove it."

The little creep started to speak, then shut up. Seconds later I felt a tap on my shoulder. I turned around and the creep was standing next to me.

He poked me with a stiff finger and said, "Do I know you, pally?"

"I kind of hope not."

"Lissen — " He started to poke me again.

"I'll break it," I said pleasantly.

"Huh? You'll what?"

"The finger. You poke me with it again and I'll break it off." I smiled at him.

He didn't smile back. But neither did he pursue the subject further. Instead he said flatly, "Next time. Next time, pally."

Then he turned, said to Adam, "That's it, huh?" and Adam said, "That's it." The unpleasant little man left.

"What was that all about?" I asked Adam.

He shrugged his wide, heavy shoulders. "Nothing I can't handle. It's not important." His tone said the subject was closed, so I left the lid on it, deposited my plate of food on the bar and followed the creep.

He walked to a blue Ford Galaxie parked in the street before an empty lot, climbed in and drove off. I saw his lights turn right on Coast Boulevard and he headed north. Nothing, maybe; but that Trouble nerve still wiggled.

Walking back I passed within a few feet of Eve. She was standing in front of a model home talking to one of the potential customers. Men and women, singly and in pairs, some with screeching children, moved in and out of the house. The man with Eve was a large chubby fellow who looked a bit like a beardless Santa Claus, a modern Santa in brown gabardine, smoking a cigarette in a short holder. They were silhouetted against a brightly lighted view window and Eve, in profile, was damn near unbelievable. I waved at her but she didn't notice me, and I went on back up by the pool.

Jim and I ate my plate of goodies, and Adam joined us for a drink. He seemed to have forgotten the peculiar altercation with Creepy and was laughing, high-spirited, his normal self again.

Adam was about my height, but even heavier than I, with big bones and big hands, a massive neck and deep chest. He was forty-one years old, his dark crew-cut flecked with gray at the temples, and with greenish-blue eyes much like Jim's. He was square-jawed, square-headed, with a face as open and honest as the plains of Texas from whence he hailed, and he looked strong enough to pick up a grown ox.

Adam and Jim made a good team. Jim, despite his penchant for high life and lovely ladies was the drive guy, the man who finished whatever he started come hell-fire or flood. Adam, though even more eager than Jim in pursuit of the female, was less intense, more relaxed, yet highly creative. "A man," Jim had told me, "with a million ideas — at least a hundred thousand of which might work." Adam had dreamed up the lighted map, the P.A. system, suggested the gals from Alexandria's, while Jim had made the ideas work, handled most of the physical details, arranged needed loans and financing.

They were not only a good team but good friends; there was an evident though not overly obvious closeness between them, an easy familiarity much like that between Jim and me.

Adam glanced at his watch. "You want to close up tonight, Jim?" he asked. "Or have Wally do it? I've got a date."

"Sure." Jim grinned. "I'll have Wally do it."

Adam said, "You're a sly one, James," and waved a hand. "See you tomorrow." He nodded at me, said, "Glad you could make it out here, Shell," and left.

As he walked away Jim glanced around. The crowd was thinning out. "Looks as if we might swing it this time, hey, Shell? If it goes like this another week or two . . . Well, it'll feel damned good."

I knew what he meant. I wasn't aware of how much money Adam had contributed to the project, but I did know Jim had poured in every cent he owned, plus mountainous mortgages, and if Laguna Paradise flopped, Jim would go down with it. Right now, though, on the sixth day of the operation, it looked like a sure winner.

Jim stretched, then frowned and said, "What in hell's happened to the gals? If I've been stood up — "

"Ha. How can you be stood up when you don't have a date yet?"

He glowered, then his gaze went past me and his face lighted up, and I guessed, correctly, that he'd seen Eve and Laurie approaching.

The girls marched up to us and said in unison, "*Why not?*"

Well, friends, unless you have heard at least one tomato as well-ripened as these crying with gay abandon, "*Why not?*" you won't know what I'm talking about — and maybe it's just as well. But the total atmosphere changed in that one twanging moment. If you still don't know what I'm talking about, try jumping from a cold shower into a hot tub.

"Hey-hey," said Jim eagerly. "This is sure the night for it!"

"For what?" Laurie asked, perhaps a bit dubiously.

"Well, ah . . . ah . . ." said Jim.

"I'm with you," Eve said, smiling more broadly than I'd ever seen her smile before. Then she put her hands on her ample hips, and pulled her shoulders back, straining the sweater dangerously, as if aiming at us. Hell, even to an *innocent* bystander it would have been an obvious act of deliberate aiming, and Jim, unashamedly staring, pushed me aside as though to accept the whole charge himself and cried, "To hell with the blindfold!"

For a second or two I thought he was going to charge forward like the Light Brigade and hurl himself upon the cannons, but instead he spun around once in a speedy circle and then said, "Well, we all have to drive back to L. A. tonight, anyway. My place sort of hangs over the Sunset Strip. How about a late supper there?"

"Sounds fun," Eve said, and Laurie chimed in, "Fine."

Jim went on, "Then, after chow, we can do something jolly, like — well, we can work out chess problems, or read Proust to each other, or play cards. . . . "

Eve smiled. "Cards. And you live over the Sunset Strip." She glanced at Laurie. "Honey, what do you bet they suggest Sunset-Strip poker?"

I could feel something steamy creeping up on me. It was blood. "Hoo!" I said. "Laurie, I have a full house!"

"But I've got a straight flush," she laughed.

"We've got this thing backwards — "

"Who cares?" interrupted Jim. "How can you lose?"

Laurie, I was pleased to note, was laughing, her brown eyes wide and bright. Eve, also laughing, cried, "I'll raise!"

"Yeah!" Jim yelled. "*Yah!* Why not?"

People were looking at us by now. Some were even getting the hell away from the area, and one old gal about a hundred and forty years old was eyeballing us with her gums going up and down.

"Well," I said, "we've raised hell already. Guess there isn't much left to do."

"I'll bet there is," Eve said. "Let's try to think of something." The look in those pale green eyes said she'd thought of a thing or two all by herself.

It steamed on for another couple of minutes, and we agreed to meet later. Both girls had driven from the city, Eve in her white T-Bird and Laurie in her little red MG, so they suggested we all go our separate ways and they'd join us at Jim's. Eve suggested midnight, so it was to be the witching hour. Without witches.

After the girls took off, Jim lifted what was left in his glass and said, "Here's to success."

"May you sell lots of lots."

He grinned. "That, too. Wow, how about Eve? For six days I've been yakking it up with her, but it was like melting a glacier with matches. She looks — well, you've seen her. But it was freeze and chill until tonight."

"Something sure defrosted her."

"Persistence. Positive thinking. A good fairy. Who cares? Man, when she got off that gag about Sunset-Strip poker, I almost swallowed my tobacco. At least, I guess it was a gag." He raised a quizzical eyebrow. "You don't suppose she was serious, do you?"

"I don't suppose. Probably just conversation. Uh, don't you suppose?"

"I wonder," he said. "I wonder. . . . "

As a matter of fact, I wondered, too. All the way home.

11

Three

It takes only an hour to get from Laguna to Los Angeles on the Santa Ana Freeway and I'd left well before ten, so by eleven-fifteen that balmy P.M. I was driving my convertible Cadillac up the Sunset Strip, top down, breeze cooling my freshly showered, shaved, and after-shave-scented chops.

Decked out resplendently — I thought — in creamy-beige silk-gabardine slacks, white jacket cut to conceal the slight bulge of my .38 Colt Special nestled between jacket and white shirt, and wearing a blazing peacock-colored necktie, I felt ready to grapple with anything the evening might offer. Though I didn't really expect to need the gun.

Jim lived on the high side of Forest Knoll Drive, well above street level, in a low and modern eight-room house which jutted from the side of a steeply sloping hill and was supported on the downhill side by thick concrete pillars. It seemed to float in the air like a huge wing, high over the Sunset Strip, and on a clear night the view of the city's lights spread out below was dazzling. Because of the location, there was plenty of seclusion and privacy, and the land was so thickly land-scaped and overgrown it would discourage the most prying eyes.

I drove up Sunset Plaza Drive, turned off on Forest Knoll, and parked on Laurel at the foot of a long flight of wooden steps which led up to Jim's place, then started climbing them. At the top of the steps was a gently sloping earthen path which ended before a ramp curving up to both the big wooden deck in front of the house and a side door which opened into Jim's sunken living room. As I started up the dirt path, a movement on my left caught my eye.

The area here was lush with shrubs and tropical plants, ferns and elephant ears, philodendron and birds of paradise. Ahead and on my left was a clump of three Senegal date palms, and that's where I thought something had moved.

"Jim?" I called. "That you?"

There wasn't any answer — but something moved there, for sure. More quickly now. And away from me. Squinting, I could see it was a man's figure, a man bent over and starting to trot toward the narrow street behind Jim's house.

"Hold it!" I yelled — and at that moment light spilled from the side of the house. I heard Jim's voice calling something. He'd opened the door up there and light from inside brightened the area — but it fell on me, not the other man, and I could barely see him, now.

"Hold it!" I yelled again, and the guy started running as if pursued by the hounds of hell. He *was* pursued, at least briefly, by me. I leaped forward and my foot skidded on slick grass. My feet went up, and I went down. By the time I got to my feet and started sprinting forward I could hear the sound of the man running well ahead of me. Then the quick slap-slap of shoe leather on paving, the sudden sound of a car's acceleration, and then the car door slamming. I reached the street in time to see the flare of taillights, then the car was gone.

As I walked up the ramp Jim said, "What the hell was that?"

"You know as much as I do," I said. "You see the guy?"

"Just a glimpse. Any idea who he was?"

I shook my head.

We didn't get anywhere guessing about the man, so we dropped it and went inside. Soft music from hidden speakers throbbed in the air. From the door, three carpeted steps led down into the living room. It extended almost the entire width of the house, to a wall paneled in pecky cedar, beyond which was the master bedroom. On the left, two wide and curving steps rose to an area that while actually part of the living room seemed separate from it. The area was furnished with an off-white divan slanted near a fireplace, a hanging pierced-metal lamp that looked Persian, a low bar in dark wood, another off-white overstaffed chair, and four big brightly-colored "harem" pillows on the floor.

"Now that you've caught your breath," Jim said, "I have a drink that'll take it away."

I grinned. "What's it called? Halitosis?"

"No, this is my special Martini — you don't stir the gin and get it all diluted with water, and you use vodka instead of vermouth. Or would you prefer a Blastoff?"

"I doubt it. It sounds like a Russian corporal — "

"Not at all. It's one part Kahlua and four parts kerosene."

"That's a *drink*?"

"Of course not. You just light it and watch it burn. But obviously you're a man who can't make a decision. I shall therefore give you one of my Martinis in a beer mug, which will render all decisions academic."

We perched on stools at the bar, and I discovered Jim really had made his special Martinis, poured the poison into two one-quart champagne bottles and inserted the bottles into silver wine buckets filled with crushed ice.

"Suppose the girls don't like undiluted gin-vodka Martinis?" I commented.

"Then these are all for us," he said sadly. "Or, I shall tell them it's very cheap champagne, the kind that doesn't tickle. Cheers."

We drank. It wasn't bad, I guessed. It wasn't good, either. In fact, I decided, it was lousy.

I had another sip, and *bang*, out of nowhere, I placed a face. Earlier I had unsuccessfully squeezed my mind trying to remember who was the guy I'd seen talking to Adam Preston. As so often happens when you worry an idea and then drop it out of mind, it had sprung back into consciousness when I least expected it.

It had been years since I'd seen those cold eyes and pinched features, but now I remembered them — and his name. Mickey M. he was called among the light-fingered lads and the boys on the heavy. Some years ago in L. A. there'd been a loosely-knit gang of heist men and hop-heads engaged in making a fast buck from whatever was illicit, four or five crumbs headed by a mugg named Lou the Greek. Two of the others were Mickey M. and Anthony "Ants" Cini. It was possible that Mickey had gone legit since then, but most underworld cats, like leopards, never change their spots, and it was a solid bet that Adam's acquaintance was still on the turf.

I said to Jim, "Do you know if Adam has ever been mixed up with guys in rackets?"

He looked startled. "What the hell kind of question is that? What brought this on?"

I told him what I knew about Mickey M., mentioned seeing him with Adam earlier, and repeated what I'd heard of their conversation. "I don't know what it was all about," I said, "but the little guy was talking pretty big. It's just a thought, Jim, but a multi-million-dollar operation like Laguna Paradise is the kind of thing today's muscle boys would love to muscle in on."

Jim was frowning, silent for a few seconds. Then he said, "He mentioned Brea? This little guy?"

"Yeah. That's all I heard, just the word. Or name. Mean anything to you?"

Jim's face smoothed. "Probably Brea Island."

"What's Brea Island?"

"A little island off the coast about fifty miles. As you know, Shell, if the Laguna project pans out it'll be the first in a series of similar developments. There'll be one in Baja California, a Monterey Paradise, maybe one down near Torrey Pines. And then there's the one I'd really like to do — Paradise Island." He looked past me, silent for a moment as he thought about it. "It'd be on Brea, big hotel, pools, beaches, cabañas, there's even room for a golf course and a little bay where we could build slips for pleasure boats."

"You own this island?"

"No, but Adam does. When he showed up last October, when we met I mean, he'd just bought it. Didn't have any special plans for it, but when he came in with me on the Laguna thing we got to talking about developing the island." He grinned. "If we didn't go broke in Laguna first, that is. I went out there with him a couple times and looked it over, and Adam's spent a lot of time there the last few months. He really got steamed up about it — even had a crew of men with him for a while, surveying, clearing a section away, building a little shack. Anyway, that could be the next project: Paradise Island. How does it sound?"

"Great. Save me a cabaña for the opening. But what's that got to do with Mickey M.?"

"Maybe nothing, except you say he mentioned Brea. He must have been talking about the island." Jim frowned. "Funny thing, last Sunday, when we opened the Laguna development, there was a guy out there in the afternoon talking to Adam about the island. Trying to get him to sell it to him."

"A guy like Mickey M.?"

Jim laughed. "Hardly. This was a real harmless-looking old duck named Lorimer, Horace Lorimer."

"What did this Lorimer want it for?"

"He's got some kind of factory out there, on the north end of the island. I gather — "

"Just a minute. A factory — on an *island?* What in hell kind of factory, what do they manufacture?"

"It's some kind of food-processing plant. Handi-Foods, Inc., I think it's called."

"Handi-Foods . . . on an island, huh? Goofy. How in hell do they ship the product? Do the workers live on the island, or what?"

"Lorimer's got a yacht, converted for carrying the product into ports along the coast here, and I think most of the workers stay out there during the week, go back and forth on a company boat when necessary. I'm not too sure how they operate, I never saw the factory. But Adam was over there a few times, so he could tell you more about it if you're curious."

"I'm curious. You say Lorimer was talking to you and Adam about the island last Sunday?"

"Not to me, just Adam. They were alone in one of the model homes and I heard part of the discussion before I stepped inside." He squinted. "They shut up when I came in — kind of odd, now that I think about it. Anyway, I mentioned it to Adam later and he said when he bought the island the deal included leasing the north half — the part the factory's on — to Lorimer, or to his corporation. So the man could stay in business, apparently. But now Lorimer's interested in buying the rest of the land, owning the whole island outright. Well, there's only an oral agreement between Adam and me, nothing on paper, that is, and after all the island is his — he can do whatever he wants with it. But he told me he had no intention of selling, even for a good profit, as long as we had plans to develop that south half of Brea."

I had another sip of my Martini — or whatever it was — and seriously wondered if my tongue was dissolving. Then I said, "Well, it would be interesting to know what connection, if any, this has with Mickey M. — "

Jim interrupted, "Oh, the hell with Mickey M. I'm in no mood for him, pal. Tonight I'm in the mood for . . ." He paused, seeking the appropriate phrase. As if to supply it, right then the chimes went off, three notes rising in jolly pitch: bing-bong-*clong!*

I looked at my watch. Ten minutes to midnight. One of the girls was eager. I was glad.

Jim said, "I'll get it!"

"Maybe it's for me."

"Ha!" he said, strode to the door and flung it open. "Darling!" he cried. "You came back!" He babbled on for a bit, some nonsense about his being sorry he'd beaten her for burning the toast, then stopped. "What's the matter? You can come in, dear." He paused. "Really."

It had been quite a while, and I was wondering who the devil was out there. Then, finally, Eve stepped inside, undulated past Jim, spotted me and waved, aimed a thumb at Jim and tapped her head. I nodded, tapping my head. Jim escorted Eve to the bar, slipped a lightweight orange coat from her shoulders, then stepped back and admired her with his eyes and with pursed lips through which he whistled an admiring whistle.

Understandably. There is a cloth called jersey, from which women's garments are sometimes made, and jersey clings to skin like skin does to nudists, and Eve was wearing jersey. The dress was bright orange, a simple one-piece cocktail dress scooped out deeply at the neck — scooped so deeply, in fact, that it was hard to decide whether it was simply falling down or whether Eve had started to take the thing off. It was a grand dress, I thought.

Jim said, "Lady, I should wash out my eyes with soap. You are absolutely gorgeous."

Smiling, Eve delicately touched her gleaming, perfectly set black hair, and thanked him. Then she said, "What's that? Champagne?" looking at the poisoned champagne bottles.

"Well . . . not exactly," Jim said. "Are you game?"

She looked at Jim and smiled, slanted her green eyes briefly toward me, then back at Jim. "I'm game," she said. That was all. Two words. Practically a book.

Jim poured from the bottle into a champagne glass and Eve took a delicate sip, then grimaced indelicately. "What the hell?" she said. Then, "Oops."

"Good, huh?" Jim said, grinning.

"Oh, marvelous." She paused. "Is it hydrochloric acid?"

"I'll fix something else, if you'd like."

"This is fine. It doesn't matter, anyway. Something else would only taste like this now."

We all sipped and went "Haah!" and talked it up a bit, then: bing-bong-*clong*.

"I'll get it," I said.

When I opened the door and saw Laurie, everything that had happened to my nervous system the first time I saw her happened again. She wore a black dress with a "V" neckline, and looped behind her neck was the thin strap of what is called a "halter," though the name conveys an entirely erroneous impression since the halter was doing very little halting. I simply looked at her silently, not saying a word. It was, indeed, a face to stop a heart, and a body to start it again.

Finally she said, "Well, shoot, you don't remember me."

That snapped me out of it. "Sure I do," I said smiling. "You're . . . ah, uh . . . You're Lucy — no, Annie . . . Arly? Cathy? Rachel? Joy?" I paused. "Francine? Frank? Bill?"

"That's who," she said smiling, and swept past me as I stepped aside, still puzzling over her name.

Soon the four of us were at the bar, and Laurie — by this time forewarned of what she was about to sink her teeth into, and what was about to sink into her teeth — had sipped the cocktail and was saying, "Ack, wonderful. Isn't it, ack, wonderful?" while making ghastly faces and shaking her head back and forth vigorously.

"Kind of strong, huh?" I said to her.

She looked straight at me, then let her eyes slowly cross. "I have been bitten by a gin snake," she said, "with vermouth fangs."

"No vermouth," Jim said brightly.

"Jim," I said, "maybe we should switch to Blastoffs."

"No, not that. But — I have it. Ladies, how about vodka poured over hot rocks? You drink the steam with your nose."

"It's a gasser," I said.

"I'll try a snort," Laurie said, and Eve merely finished her Gintini, or whatever it was. But then she'd had a ten-minute head start on Laurie. Jim generously refueled her glass.

Well, we each had three of those things, so when Jim said, "What say we eat?" Laurie cried, "Why not?" and Eve said, "Ah, pour me an appetizer first," and I said, "Drink up before the glasses crack."

And Jim went on, "Everybody relax." And I let air bubble happily from my lips, and Eve yawned hugely, and Laurie slid gently to the floor, and Jim continued as if nothing had happened, "Because *I* am going to prepare our supper. And, kids, it is going to be a flaming supper. Isn't that exciting?"

"Go ahead and bum it," Eve said.

"In paper plates," Laurie said. "I'll scrape up the dishes."

Jim sprang from the bar and busied himself somewhere out of sight, then called to me to help him carry a variety of objects back to the girl area. In a few moments we were all sitting comfortably on the floor, on the harem pillows, and Jim went to work.

Despite all the horsing around, that after-midnight supper was extraordinarily good. Jim fixed everything at the table — or rather the floor — in chafing dishes, and not only was it all delicious but he put on quite a show as well.

We started with a creamy hot cheese fondue into which we dunked chunks of day-old French bread torn from a huge loaf, went on to a spicy soup, and then another fondue in which large juicy morsels of filet mignon steamed and sizzled, and wound up with ambrosial *crêpes suzette*. As a finale Jim poured a bit of Remy Martin cognac into brandy snifters, rolled the liquor around to coat their insides, lighted them, let the flickering blue flames heat the snifters, then poured a healthy dollop of brandy into each glass. With that food inside us, and sipping the warm liquor, it was not surprising that we were wrapped in an aura of almost sinful luxuriousness. Or luxurious sinfulness. Whatever it was, it was good.

After accepting rhapsodic compliments on his culinary prowess, Jim said, "Now, friends, the movies."

Every hair on my head, neck and ears, sprang to uneasy attention. I followed Jim to a closet from which he took a sixteen-millimeter projector and screen, and said to him, feeling more than a bit uneasy, "What's this? Jim, what's this?"

He merely smiled and said all would soon be clear.

That's what I was afraid of. Not that it was *absolutely* out of the question; but you just *don't* go tossing things like that at people without suitable preparation. As Jim set up the screen and projector, I said to him suspiciously, "Movies?"

"Yeah, movies," he said brightly.

"What kind of movies?" I asked, even more suspiciously.

"You'll see," he said.

I knew Jim was an expert photographer, and that both still and movie photography were among his numerous hobbies. Maybe these were home movies of his trip to Hawaii. Only he hadn't made any trip to Hawaii.

I was sure of it. I was appalled. I just knew, when the picture flickered on the screen, there would be a droopily mustached Latin character fidgeting about and peeking through a window at a shapely tomato doing something horrible, I just knew it.

With me sort of dragging my feet, we trooped into the living room carrying our big pillows and got settled. Jim turned out the lights, turned on the projector, and said, "This is a mm I made myself."

"You *what?*" I said, aghast.

"Made it myself," he said happily. "I'll bet you find this interesting."

"Yeah," I said. "I'll bet."

Then I turned to look, eyes wide and watery, at the screen.

Four

At first I couldn't figure out what was on the screen, but almost immediately my uneasiness left me, though it was replaced by perplexity. Because whatever this was, it was at least not what I'd been imagining.

Then Jim started explaining, and it made sense, and I — all of us, I think — began really enjoying the film.

"This," Jim explained, "is time-lapse photography. I set up a movie camera and tripod on the deck, aimed it over the Sunset Strip down below us, and rigged it with a timer so one frame of film would be exposed every fifteen seconds."

He went on to explain that normally movie film is taken at a speed of 16 frames per second and also projected at that speed, thus exactly reproducing whatever movement the lens captured. But for Jim's film only four frames had been exposed during each minute of the day and night, though the developed film would be run at the normal speed of 16 frames per second. Thus, while it required four hours to expose 960 frames, that length of film would run through the projector in one minute. Or, to put it another way, into one minute of viewing time was compressed four hours of the day.

Merely to hear Jim explain it wasn't very interesting, but the sight itself on the screen was fascinating, more so with each minute that passed.

The things which remained motionless for more than fifteen seconds naturally were captured on more than one frame of film, so trees, buildings, parked cars, were recognizable. But moving cars were merely dots or blurs; little puppet-people danced about like jumping fleas. Jim had used a wide-angle lens on his camera, so not

21

only was the ground immediately below us visible but also the sky above. And probably most strange and interesting of all was the sight of that living, boiling sky, and the sensation it gave of the weird acceleration of time. It was night; then suddenly it was day, the sky brightened. Clouds raced over the blue, formed swiftly and dissolved just as quickly, bunched into masses, then thinned and disappeared. The light softened, and night fell with a rush. The Sunset Strip itself wasn't visible from here, but other streets were thin arteries with lights streaking both ways along them, and a traffic light at the screen's right flickered in a faint pattern of reds and greens with an occasional quick flash of yellow. The sun rose and set three times while we watched, the moon sailed across the screen, stars wheeled through the dark sky.

Then the film came to an end. Jim nipped on the lights.

"That was marvelous," Laurie said. "And, you know, if you'd told me what it was going to be, I probably wouldn't have been interested in seeing it."

"That's why I didn't tell you," Jim said. He looked at me, grinning, proof that he had known all along what was giving me fits, and said, "Now the movies I smuggled out of Tijuana."

"No!" I yelled.

But the girls laughed, and Jim said he was only kidding, and we went back up to the floor near the bar and had a drink. Normal drinks this time, bourbon and water for Jim and me, brandy Alexanders for Laurie and Eve.

Something was bothering me though. Something in that film we'd just seen . . . or maybe it was a feeling I'd gotten earlier, talking to Jim about Laguna Paradise, Brea Island, and Adam, that Jim had been holding something back, not telling me everything. Whatever the reason, a prickle of uneasiness kept sticking me. But the conversation zipped along dandily, and my uneasiness ebbed. We were having a ball, we were all marvelously relaxed. . . .

I don't really know how it happened.

All I remember is that in the middle of one of Jim's stereo albums was an old oldie, "Strip Polka," and that lit the fuse for several more comments, and suddenly Jim had a deck of cards in his hands and was shuffling them. Oddly enough, Eve, who had broadly hinted at such an eventuality earlier in the evening, seemed even more reticent than

Laurie now, and resisted quite a bit of coaxing from Jim — and, I'll admit it, from me — but finally, when Laurie merrily repeated that phrase often heard for the first time in grammar school, "I will if you will," Eve took a deep breath, aimed, practically fired, and said, "I'm trapped. I'm trapped. So deal."

Jim dealt.

The way Jim was playing the game, there was no ante, and only the high hand was not required to pay a forfeit, while all three other gamblers were required, in poker vernacular, to "sweeten the pot" As luck would have it, Laurie won every one of the first three hands.

Jim and I lost our shoes and jackets but were in no immediate danger, since we had slyly begun the game with several more articles of apparel than either of the girls. This became rather startlingly apparent after the third hand, since Eve had already lost both shoes, and she was wearing no hose. So. . . .

"My goodness," she said, looking at Laurie. "You haven't lost *any*thing, have you?"

"No," Laurie squealed. She looked at me, laughing, her brown eyes sparkling. "Not a *thing*."

"Bah," I said.

"Eve, quit stalling," Jim said in mock savagery.

"Oh, dear," she said. And for perhaps five long seconds there was a sticky silence. Then she scooted nearer Laurie and whispered in her ear. I thought: What's she saying? But then Eve turned her back to Laurie, who deftly unhooked something, and then pulled a long zipper down, down, down. . . .

There is no sound like that sound. None.

Then Eve stood up, lifted her hands to her shoulders, and in a moment the orange dress slid slowly down her arms, over her breasts, slipped past her hips and crumpled in bright disarray on the floor.

She stepped from the dress, and there was another silence — but not sticky this time. This time it was a charged, pulsing, electric silence that crackled almost audibly. Eve, in the outfit worn by the girls at Laguna Paradise, had been an eye-socking sight; but now, in a low pale-pink brassiere and brief bikini-like step-ins, she was damn near blinding. Eve was a vast expanse of lovely white flesh, her near nakedness interrupted only by the wisp of pink at her hips and another bit of pink partially concealing those superbly abundant breasts. Partially concealing, for above the pink cloth mounds of creamy whiteness rose in swollen voluptuousness.

Eve sat down again, folding her long legs beneath her, white flesh trembling. Then she leaned toward Laurie, rested a hand gently on her thigh, and said, "You'd better lose pretty soon, honey." And she smiled a very enticing smile. So she was smiling at Laurie, of course, but at least she was *smiling*. She might have let out a high scream and wailed, "I can't go on," whereupon, at this point, both Jim and I might have dived off the deck onto our heads.

But after that one moment of silence — that moment of truth, so to speak — there was merely an inaudible snap-crackle-and-pop in the electric air, and the conversation ripped easily along.

"Gimme the cards," I said.

"Deal!" said Jim.

I shuffled grimly, looked at Laurie. "Lose!" I said.

She cocked her blonde head to one side, looking very cute, stuck out her tongue and said sweetly, "I'll try."

"Five-card stud," I said, and dealt the first card face down, the next one up. I had a king in the hole, a queen on the top. My next card was a queen, the fourth a deuce, the last a king. Two pair. Jim had a pair of sevens showing, Eve a possible straight, and Laurie four hearts.

Then we turned up our hole cards.

Laurie turned up a club — nothing. "Ah-ha!" I said.

Jim had a pair of sevens. And Eve's hole card filled her straight.

So I lost a sock. So what? Laurie supped off a shoe. A step in the right direction.

Eve won the next hand, too. Another sock — my feet were bare. And Laurie contributed a second shoe. Laurie, I had noted, wore no hose, either.

It was Eve's deal again. She shuffled, dealt five cards for draw poker. We drew, and I wound up with my best hand of the night, three kings.

"Oh, dear," Eve said. And, "Oh, oh," said Laurie.

"Aces up," Jim said.

Then I showed my three kings. Neither of the girls had even a pair. I'd won.

Jim unbuttoned his shirt, saying, "When do I win a hand?" and Laurie and Eve looked at each other.

Laurie said, "I might as well say it — you'll know soon enough, anyway. I'm . . . not wearing a brassiere."

That was good.

Eve glanced at the ceiling, then said to Laurie, "Well, I'll zip you, honey."

"The word," I said, "is *unzip*."

Laurie glanced at me, her mouth round, her honey-brown eyes wide and bright. She turned sideways and Eve did the unhook-and-zip bit, and the sound literally sizzled. Eve turned her back to Laurie and said, "Your turn, Sweetie," and Laurie unhooked those tricky little businesses. As the last hook parted, the pink cloth fell away from Eve's skin a little. Just a little. She moved back to her pillow, faced us. Laurie ducked her head, pulled the strap from behind her neck and over her blonde hair, then put her hands at the top of the dress.

Eve shrugged her white shoulders and the pink bra fell downward of its own weight, came to rest in her lap. Her breasts quivered momentarily, quivered and then became still. She picked up the bra, dropped it to one side — but by then I was watching Laurie.

Laurie looked straight at me, eyes slightly narrowed, ran her tongue over her lower lip. Then she arched her back, breasts thrusting forward, and moved the black cloth down. And the phone rang.

Laurie jumped, but it was nothing to my jump. If it could have been measured it would surely have been a new record from a standing sit, or whatever it was. From absolutely immobile rigidity I went at least two feet in the air.

"What in the hell?" said Jim.

"It's nothing," I said rapidly. "Nothing. Probably somebody's alarm clock — " And the phone rang again.

Laurie was motionless, the dress lowered a few inches, two swelling mounds of white and a small arc of pink pressing against the black cloth.

The phone shrilled again . . . and again.

"Hell," Jim said, "hold everything." He got up, went to the phone. "Yeah, hello?" he said.

The phone was up here near us, on a stand against the wall, and I could see Jim's face as he listened silently. Laurie said, questioningly, "Saved by the bell?" but something had already gone out of the

25

evening. She tugged upward at the neck of her dress, and Eve, I noticed, was putting her brassiere back on.

Then I saw Jim's face. He paled as I watched him. His jaw sagged and he put out one hand as if to steady himself. He mumbled something into the phone, then hung up. He just stood there.

"Jim," I said, "what's the matter? What is it?"

"Adam's dead."

"Dead? What — how, Jim?"

"He's dead." His face was twisted; he seemed in shock. "Adam's dead. Shot. Murdered."

Five

I parked the Cad in front of Adam Preston's house. Two police cars were at the curb ahead of us. Jim had come with me, but he'd spoken hardly at all on the way.

I said to him, "Jim this is bad, I know. But pull yourself together. When we get in there . . ." I stopped. "How come they called you? Could it have anything to do with Laguna — "

"No." He interrupted me. "I — " He stopped, swallowed and sighed heavily. "You see, Shell, his name isn't really Adam. It's Aaron." He looked straight at me. "Aaron Paradise. He's my brother."

Jim got out of the car before I could say anything in reply. Silently we walked up to the front door. A uniformed officer stood there. He was expecting us, and we went in.

A plainclothes lieutenant named Wesley Simpson was in the living room, jotting something in a notebook. He turned, nodded to me, and said, "Be with you in a minute, Shell."

Jim stood next to me, arms hanging at his sides, his face still looking bleached. I put my hand on his arm. "Jim — "

He shook his head. "Later, Shell."

Simpson snapped his notebook shut and walked over to us. He nodded to me then looked at Jim. "You're Mr. Paradise?" They spoke briefly, then another officer led Jim through a door in the far wall. Obviously the police knew Jim was the dead man's brother. Which meant they also knew the dead man was Aaron Paradise. I wondered if that was why Jim had told me Adam was his brother — because the police already knew.

Simpson had stayed here with me. He was a solid man, thirty-eight years old, always neatly dressed. Now his eyes were a little bloodshot and the lids looked heavy — probably from lack of sleep. It was well after midnight and the Hollywood Division would be closed, the men off watch, so the first officers here would have been from the Detective Headquarters Division downtown; but they would have notified the Homicide team from Hollywood, including Simpson.

"You look beat, Wes," I said.

"I was just taking off my pants when the call came in," he said. "So sleepy I damn near came here without putting them back on. It's been a rough week."

"What's the situation?"

"Victim's still here, in the bedroom. We're just finishing up."

"He was shot, right?"

"You get a cigar. Left side, a contact wound, killed instantly. Bullet drilled right into his heart. No sign of struggle, which isn't surprising, since we figure he must have been sound asleep. He was nude in bed, which also figures — looks like he'd been having a . . . well, a party earlier. Gal left, and he conked right out. We figure the killer waited till Paradise was alone, and sleeping pretty good after the, uh, party, then let himself in and shot him."

"Let himself in? Any signs of forcible entry?"

"No, but it's a simple lock. A pro could just walk right in. Paradise didn't let him in, though. You got that?"

I nodded. "He wouldn't have gone to the door and let anybody in — not nude — and then gone back to bed. So he was shot, while asleep in bed, by somebody who picked the lock. Or had a key," I added as an afterthought.

"You get a cigar."

"How come you knew his name was Paradise, Wes? He used the name Adam Preston."

"Didn't know at first. Old Rosie was the first Homicide detective here. He remembered the dead guy's face from when he was in the Bunco section, but the name didn't fit. He checked with R and I and got the dope. And the brother's address."

Things were coming at me too fast. I said, "R and I? Paradise didn't have a record, did he?"

"Yeah, he fell from here, Shell. Did a bit in San Quentin, fifty-nine to sixty. Went to Q in January of fifty-nine."

"What'd he fall for?"

"Larceny, grand theft. Specific count was selling phony oil stocks —
the only oil was in the ink on the paper. But he also sold goldless
gold mines, underwater real estate, and one radio-unactive Alaskan
uranium mine."

"The con," I said slowly. "The big con."

"Including boiler rooms, phony paper, the whole bit." He paused,
then said, "What's the matter?"

I shook my head. "Nothing." I hoped it was nothing. I had been
thinking about all that razzle-dazzle at Laguna Paradise . . . the P.A.
system and jazz, the big map, the luscious gals, the come-on . . . the
arc lights and booze and speculative frenzy in the air. I felt sure Jim
wouldn't be party to anything crooked — to a con — but even though
the property was damned good property in one of the most desirable
locations on the coast, and being sold at an honest price, there was
still a kind of something-for-nothing pitch in the way the development was being promoted. And something-for-nothing is the rock-
solid basis of every con game ever played on a mark.

I remembered Jim's telling me most of those ideas had been Adam's
— or, rather, Aaron's. But I pushed those angles out of my mind for
now and said, "What makes you think he was having a party?"

"Looks like some gal had been here. Glasses for drinks, little smear
of lipstick on one, a couple short blonde hairs on the pillow. Another
thing — try this one, Shell."

"O.K."

"Well, he was very neat. Clothes all on shaped hangers, shoe trees
in the shoes, everything — even socks — folded real neat in the draw-
ers, you know. Well, he's in bed, nude like I said, and the clothes he
was wearing are just tossed on a chair — or at it. All in a mess, one
trouser leg inside out and so on. Guy like that, he hangs up his clothes,
unless — "

I nodded. "O.K., so he wasn't worried about hangers right then, or
shoe trees. I'll buy the party."

"You get a ci — "

"What about the girl? Anyone see her?"

"No. All we know about her is she must be a hot-pants blonde.
Account of the blonde hairs on the pillow." He made a sour face.
"Unless they were left over from the night before?"

"Maybe the whole party was from the night before?"

29

"Doesn't figure that way, not along with all the rest of it."

He was right. And, too, I remembered Aaron's asking Jim to close up at Laguna, saying he had a date. I asked Wes, "What time did it happen?"

"Just after midnight." He consulted his notebook, flipped a couple of pages. "Call came in to the complaint board at twelve-ten A.M. Man reported he'd just heard a shot and gave the address."

"How come he could pin the location down so close?"

"Claimed he was a neighbor. Wasn't sure of the address, but thought it came from here or the next house. Officers in the car answering the call checked both houses and found the victim here. He was still warm, blood still wet on him."

"Who was the guy that called in?"

Wes flipped his notebook shut. "Didn't give his name. Same old story, another good citizen who didn't want to get involved."

"Yeah."

Jim came back, slumped in a chair and pressed his face into his hands. Wes asked me if I wanted to look at the scene of the crime and I nodded. He led me into the bedroom.

One last photographic bulb flashed as we went inside. Everything was as Wes had described it for me, so there wasn't much to see — except the ugliness of violent death. Aaron lay on his back in bed, his big strong body nude, head far to one side. The clothes Wes had mentioned were more neatly stacked now, since the police had probably gone through the pockets, then placed the garments on the chair. Two partly filled highball glasses sat on the bed's wooden headboard.

"Brandy and soda," Wes said. "Not that it means anything. No prints on the glasses, either, so that's no help. They've been wiped clean, along with the front doorknob, outside and inside. No prints here except the victim's."

I took a last look at the victim, the late Aaron Paradise, lately Adam Preston. The lethal bullet had entered his left side and smashed the heart, but his heart must have pumped spasmodically once or twice before it stopped. There was a large stain of red on the white sheet beneath him, a suprisingly large stain.

I told Wes I'd be in touch, thanked him for filling me in, and walked out.

Jim and I sat in my car, parked in front of his brother's home. The police had gone. Jim was still shaken, but he was in better shape, more in control, now. He asked me to do what I could, try to find out who had killed Aaron — and why — and insisted that it be handled as investigator and client, for my usual fee plus quite a bit more, win or lose. He knew I'd go all out because we were close friends, if he merely asked me; but he wanted it his way, and I told him all right.

We were long-time friends, but he'd never mentioned having a brother. I remembered that earlier I'd felt he was holding something back. Now I knew what it had been. I'd been uneasy . . . but the uneasiness had started sticking me right after — or during — Jim's running of that film. And that prickly unease was still with me, still . . .

I caught the thought, held it.

In a moment I said, "Jim, I want to see that time-lapse film again."

He blinked at me. "You what?"

I started the car. "I want you to run that film for me again, the one we watched tonight."

"But why?"

"The damn thing is bugging me. Something I saw, maybe. Or thought I saw. Anyway, I want to check it."

I'd seen something, all right. But it hadn't impressed me then.

Jim and I were in the darkened living room of his home, film clicking through the projector, nearing its end. And in the lower right-hand corner of the screen, clear at the bottom — which meant it was on the street directly below Jim's home — a car was parked, and the figure of a man could be seen inside the car. Only one frame of the film had been exposed each fifteen seconds, I knew, but the man remained in the car while several frames clicked past the lens. He'd been parked there for at least twenty or thirty minutes, his face turned up toward Jim's house most of the time. Then there was a quick blur of him standing next to the car, looking up, one frame in which he was in the street walking toward the wooden steps below, and another in which just his lowered head and shoulders were visible.

I had Jim reverse the film a couple of times, running it forward again as slowly as he could past the frame in which the man stood next to his car looking up at the house.

It was unmistakable when run slowly. The man had been watching Jim's house, then walked to the wooden steps. After that point

31

he was out of sight, but he had almost surely been heading for the steps which led up to Jim's front door, and presumably had gone up those steps to the house. The figure was so small on the screen I couldn't be positive of the man's identity; but the car was a blue Ford Galaxie, and I was sure enough: Mickey M. A busy little bastard, Mickey M.

I said to Jim, "When did you make this film?"

"Started it Tuesday morning, let it run three full days, till Friday morning. Took it in for special processing Friday on the way to Laguna, and it was delivered yesterday before I got home."

"Then this creep was watching your place Thursday night — and probably came up to the house. He could have been here Friday night, too, for that matter. And eight to five he's the guy I chased out of here a few hours ago."

Jim said, "But why in hell would anybody be watching *my* place?"

"Why in bell would anybody kill Aaron?" I didn't intend for it to sound so brutal, but I went on. "The little creep doing the watching, incidentally, the guy in your film, was Mickey M."

He frowned. "The one you mentioned? Talking to Aaron?"

"The same. Jim, it's possible *both* you and Aaron were supposed to be killed tonight."

"That doesn't make sense."

"None of it makes sense. Not yet. When we know why your brother was killed, a lot of things might make sense — including why that guy was hanging around here earlier. Until then . . ." I paused. "Have you got a gun handy?"

"Couple hunting rifles. No revolver."

"I've got an old .32 Smith & Wesson in the back of the Cad. That is, if you don't mind having an ex-safecracker's gun in the house."

He shrugged. "Not that I'll need it."

"Well, the safecracker doesn't need it any more." I got to my feet. "I'll bring it up."

I found the little gun in the Cad's trunk, under a walkie-talkie and next to a spring-loaded sap, checked it to make sure it was loaded. It was. I closed the trunk, went back up the wooden steps.

I was thinking about that time-lapse film, and for a moment I had the weird feeling that time had slipped backwards, that I was reliving something that had happened before. There was this difference — the figure I saw was not on my left, but at the top of the ramp this time, standing before Jim's door. For the time it took me to move two steps forward, the sight was merely a warped moment — but then I snapped out of it, as Jim's door opened and light fell on the little man, and I saw the gleam of metal in his hand.

"Look out! Jim, look — "

That was as far as I got. The gun in the man's hand blasted and Jim jumped — or fell — back, and in almost the same instant the little guy spun around. His gun cracked and I heard the solid chunk of metal split the air near my head.

I heard the sharp crack of my own gun and felt my hand jump as the gun in it kicked before I realized I was firing. The S & W .32 had been in my hand from the time I'd left the Cad until this moment, and now it was leveled at the man and I was squeezing the trigger, squeezing it again.

The other guy didn't get off a second shot at me. He bent forward, collapsing in the middle, then started straightening up, then his body jerked twice more as slugs from the .32 slammed into him. The hammer fell on an empty cylinder and I dropped the revolver, grabbed under my coat for my own Colt Special. But it wasn't needed.

The man toppled forward, got one foot out in front of him, but the leg wouldn't hold his weight; it buckled and he fell toward me, sprawling spread-eagled on the ramp, head lower down than his feet. Light spilled from the open doorway and covered him with a faintly rosy glow.

I ran forward, leaped up the ramp and grabbed the man, yanked him over. He was alive. But not for long. He had maybe ten seconds left. His eyes wobbled, rolled, and his lips stretched apart over teeth that were tight together. Bloody froth spilled from his mouth. I could hear the little hissing sound as the fluid squeezed through his teeth and past his lips. His head jerked crazily.

Then his body straightened convulsively, arched, and his entire frame trembled, trembled horribly. A convulsive shudder ran through him and he began vibrating with an awful spasm that shook every bit of his body.

It was a frightening thing to watch. That terrible spasm couldn't have lasted long; it seemed very long to me. Then it ended. Ended suddenly, and that was all. The man lay still. He was dead.

And only then did the weird emotion, the near paralysis which had held me, loosen, let me think. I looked at him, wondering what it meant.

Even in death the features were still pinched. The eyes were still cold, but even colder and more uncommunicative now. It was the same guy. Mickey M.

Six

Since the gunshots there had been no sound. I hadn't seen Jim after that moment when he'd been in the doorway. I ran my tongue over dry lips, got to my feet.

There was a noise from inside the house. I saw Jim standing in the doorway, one hand pressed to the back of his head. Some of the tension drained out of me; he was alive.

As I walked toward him he said, "What happened? What — who was that?" He looked past me to the dead man.

I said, "Did he hit you?"

"No. You yelled, and I guess I saw the guy there at the same moment or just afterward." He felt his chest and stomach. "He didn't hit me. I don't feel anything. But I fell in there, slammed my head on something." His chest heaved. "I heard the gunshots."

We stepped inside, shut the door. I told him who the dead man was and added, "So that settles it. He was the guy watching your place, undoubtedly the man who ran out of here tonight."

Jim shook his head. "It doesn't make any, sense. It doesn't make a damn bit of sense."

"Maybe it will. At least we're not guessing now, Jim. This little sonofabitch came here to kill you. Let that sink into your head. He came here to murder you, just as your brother was murdered tonight, and there's a damned good chance he's the same bastard who did me job on Aaron."

"But why — "

"Dammit, don't ask me why." I walked toward the phone. "It could be he came here to get you, had to run when I spotted him, and because of that took care of Aaron then instead. Anyway, he came back

35

here, waited, and — when he thought I'd left — came up here to kill you." I paused, thinking. "We know he was waiting out there just now, no telling for how long. And it couldn't have been coincidence that he showed up only a few minutes after I left. No, he waited till he thought you were alone. The same way he — or somebody — waited for Aaron to be alone after midnight."

I grabbed the phone, dialed, was put through to the L.A. Police Building, reported the shooting and gave this address. Then I hung up, turned around and said, "Why didn't you tell me your brother was an ex-con?"

"Well, Shell — "

I interrupted, "And while you're at it give me the rest of it, Jim. The con games and phony stocks, the dry holes, the uranium mines. The whole pretty picture."

Jim didn't speak for a moment, and when he did his voice was a little hard. "Hold on a minute, pal. I didn't *intend* to tell you about Aaron before he was killed. I had no intention of telling a damn soul. That, I figured, was Aaron's business and mine, and nobody else's, not even yours. Since that phone call, well, I haven't been thinking about much else. Except Aaron with his blood . . ." He stopped. Then he went on, "But I was going to tell you, tell you the whole bit. You didn't think I wasn't going to, did you?"

I sighed. "I'm sorry, Jim. But this has been a helluva night. I know it's been rougher for you. But it kind of jangled my nerves, too. Not to mention damn near getting myself killed out there."

Jim's eyebrows went up a bit. "He shot at you?"

"At, yeah. Just missed my ear." I grinned, tried to keep it light. "Damn near got a piece of the right one, too. Wouldn't that have tickled Laurie?"

He smiled slightly.

"How about filling in any gaps you can?" I said. "The police will be here any minute."

"Yeah. It's about time, I guess." He lit a cigarette. "Well, here's the tale — I might as well go clear back." He dragged on the cigarette. "Mix us a couple drinks, will you?"

He talked while I poured bourbon and water over ice cubes, brought the drinks back and sat down. Jim's father, Oakley "Oak" Paradise, had been an Oklahoma oilman, a wildcatter who'd brought in a few wells while still a young man. He'd made nearly two million dollars in the big strike at Cushing near Tulsa, Oklahoma, lost most of it in dry holes scattered over Kansas and Texas, made a few hundred thousand buying and selling leases in 1926 during the boom at Seminole, Oklahoma. When he died he'd left an estate which, even after estate and inheritance taxes, provided that each of his sons would receive $150,000 on reaching twenty-one.

"Aaron was nine years older than me," Jim went on. "Forty-one to my thirty-two now. So he knew Dad longer, and better, than I did. Dad was pretty wild, he lived high, made and spent a lot of money — and I guess he drank and brawled and wenched with the best of them. Anyway, Aaron took after him, more of the wild blood in him than me, I guess. He idolized Dad — Old Oak, he always called him — so he followed in his footsteps. For a while. In college he studied geology, petroleum engineering, and girls. He flunked everything but girls — graduated magna cum laude in that subject.

"Anyway, out of college, and with his hundred and fifty thousand, he set out to be another Oak. He bought leases in Texas, drilled for oil and got a lot of dirt. Oh, he brought in a few wells that pumped maybe a hundred barrels a day, but the dry holes took all that and more. He went bust in three years." Jim swallowed at his drink, let half of it run down his throat. "So he said to hell with that noise. Aaron never liked hard work, anyway. He liked money, and soft women, but not hard work. O.K., he never drilled for oil again, but he could — later — pose as a wildcatter, a big Texas oilman, an expert, when he was . . . conning a mark. Isn't that the phrase?"

"Yeah. One of them."

"First he sold all his remaining leases, where he'd drilled dry holes. Not really illegal, he just misrepresented the situation a little. He did a lot of things, sold cars, dabbled in real estate, tried politics — ran for office and lost. Along in there, the early fifties, he got married. Cute little redhead. Very cute." He grinned. "I know; I was going with her when Aaron met her."

"Where's she now, Jim?"

"Back east someplace. It doesn't matter — the marriage only lasted a year. Darlene, that's her name, went next door one day to borrow a cup of sugar from a neighbor. Seems Aaron was there. He'd, uh, already borrowed some sugar. Right after the divorce, he printed some fancy stock certificates and sold shares in — believe it or not — the Mountain of Gold Mine. There *was* a mountain, and some fool Indians or somebody had actually named it 'Mountain of Gold,' maybe because it looked yellow in the sunset twice a year. And there was actually a mine in it. A salt mine.

"So, I suppose you could say he was only three-fourths crooked then. He claimed he never actually told anybody it was a *gold* mine. But from that point on he made it four-fourths — uranium, tungsten, diamonds, complicated stock swindles. He never used a gun, that was all. Eventually he slipped. Right into prison. When he got out he changed his name. Kept the same initials, and took the name Adam — to symbolize a new beginning, he told me. Because it *was* a new beginning, on the level. The 'square' life, he said."

When Jim said, "He never used a gun," it had reminded me of something. I said, "Just a second. Mickey M.'s gun is still out there somewhere. It could be the one used on Aaron. Police will want to check it, anyway."

I hadn't seen the gun after he'd fallen, and it might have gone off the deck. Thinking about that reminded me of something else. I banged the palm of one hand on my forehead.

"What's the matter?" Jim asked.

"This hood didn't *walk* here. He must have come in a car. I should have checked that out ten minutes ago." I swore softly and said, "Be right back."

"Shell." Jim's voice was a little tight.

"Yeah?"

"It's just sinking in. There really is a good chance that little sonofabitch killed my brother, isn't there?"

"Yeah, pretty good."

"Well, I'm glad he's dead. I'm glad you killed him. But I wish I'd done it. I wish I could have killed him."

"Don't say it, Jim." Maybe he meant it; but he hadn't seen the man die.

I went to the door, stepped out on the deck and started down the ramp toward the dead man's body. Then I stopped.

"That's funny," I said aloud, with more than a little understatement. Mickey M. was gone.

Seven

Mickey M. was no longer on the ramp.

A thick smear of blood was there. That was all. No Mickey. No gun in sight.

I heard sirens. Soon the wail droned to a stop, doors slammed.

"Jim," I called.

He came to the door behind me. "Cops here?"

"That's not why I called you. Take a look." I pointed to the ramp.

"What the hell?" he said. "You move him?"

"Nope. And he sure as hell didn't move himself. He came in a car, all right. But, apparently, not alone. Probably with six other people, including stretcher bearers." I stopped, then started swearing, not so softly this time.

"What's the matter?" Jim asked.

"When he ran out of here the first time, I heard the car take off. But there wasn't any starter growl, just the sound of acceleration and *then* a door slamming. Hell, somebody else had to be in the car then, sitting there with the motor idling. Mickey just ran up and jumped in as the guy took off. Jim, if you want to hire a detective who isn't stupid — "

"Knock it off, Shell."

Policemen appeared, in large numbers.

The numbers were large because there was, first, a radio car and two uniformed policemen, then detectives working the night watch out of Central Homicide, and after them the sleepy Homicide team from the Hollywood Division, which itself consisted of one lieutenant, two sergeants, and another uniformed policeman. It just doesn't pay to shoot anybody anywhere near Los Angeles. Not, at least, if you can help it. And the first of the Hollywood detectives to appear on the scene was the lieutenant. Wesley Simpson.

He started to speak to one of the Headquarters detectives, then spotted me near the Senegal date palms and walked toward me, moving like a man in a dream. "Didn't even get my pants off," he said. "Didn't even get inside the house. Heard the call on the radio and made a U-turn — broke the law," he added sourly. He looked around. "Where's the body?"

"Well, it was here a few minutes ago — "

"Oh — " He said a four-letter word. "Usually I enjoy gagging it up with you, Scott." Scott, not Shell, which meant he was really beat. "But believe it or not, I am supposed to be working the day watch. Now where's the stiff?"

"Wes," I said gently. "I was not gagging it up. I shot this guy — "

"You're the one shot him?"

"Yeah. And he was right there." I pointed to the smear of blood on the ramp. "I stepped inside for a minute or so, and it seemed unnecessary to lug the dead guy in there with me. When I came out a little while ago, he was gone."

"Scott," he said slowly, his voice like distant thunder, "if you are being gay — "

"Wes, please, I'm telling this as simply and accurately as I can. There's a call out already, and there's still a chance a prowl car may tag a buggy speeding from here. If there's a fresh corpse in the car, that's the one."

"You mean . . ." His voice was sort of mushy, as if his tongue was loose. ". . . after you shot him, somebody walked right in here, picked him up, and took him away? Somebody *stole* him?"

"You," I said, "get a cigar."

There was not much left of the night by the time I reached the Spartan Apartment Hotel in Hollywood. The Spartan, across from the green grounds of the Wilshire Country Club, on North Rossmore Drive, is home. More importantly at the moment, that's where my bed is. And bed is where I was ten minutes after walking in the door.

I fed the tropical fish some dry food, showered, set both alarms, and fell into the sack. I was tired, but I couldn't stop my brain from whirling like a merry-go-round. I couldn't grab any brass rings, either.

40

I tried to push it all out of my mind, but pictures kept floating before my inner eye. The men and women at Laguna Paradise, Mickey M. talking to Adam-Aaron, Eve with her bold bare breasts trembling in the soft light, and Laurie, lovely Laurie. Laurie there by the pool . . . Laurie at Jim's door . . . Laurie laughing, her eyes flashing, Laurie with her hands on the top of her dress, two mounds of white and a hint of pink, a hint of promise, against the black.

I tried to keep thinking of Laurie. But two other pictures kept pushing her away, and finally only they remained. One was Aaron Paradise on his back in bed, the red stream, of life drying on his side. The other was a man dying, teeth clenched, body jerking convulsively, trembling, shaking. . . .

Always I awaken reluctantly, but this morning I woke up asleep. The first alarm scratched at consciousness; the second clawed me out of bed. But coffee was thin plasma, new bounce from the old bean. Over my second cup I was able to think about yesterday, a yesterday that seemed like a week.

Wesley Simpson had never quite lost his temper, but if he had, he would probably never have found it again. I told him the gunman was one Mickey M. — even though I had no physical evidence to prove it. But they didn't find Mickey M. To make it perfect, they didn't find his gun, either.

Jim Paradise had finished telling me his tale. His brother had wound up in prison, but Jim had done very well with his 150 G's, investing in real estate, buying apartment houses, improving them and trading or selling, whichever afforded him the bigger tax break; then investing in raw land and housing developments. With a pile of cash he'd come to California seven years ago — shortly before I'd met him at a Hollywood party — chunked it into real estate, doubled and tripled his capital. He started buying land in and around Laguna Beach and formed "Paradise Properties, Incorporated." Then this last October brother Aaron had showed up, big as life and even lustier. After a happy reunion, Jim invited Aaron to join him in the big project, which had then become Laguna Paradise. Aaron had fifty thousand dollars in cash, the title to Brea Island, and "a million ideas" — some of which produced the Barnum-type promotion I'd witnessed last night.

That was all of it. Then: Murder.

I carried a third cup of coffee into the living room of my three-rooms-and-bath, flopped on the chocolate-brown divan in front of the fake fireplace, and plunked the phone on my chest. I dialed Jim's home, and he answered on the second ring.

"Shell, Jim," I said. "How soon will you be ready?"

"Not till about nine. What say I meet you at your place then? We can leave from there."

"Fine."

Last night we had decided to go in Jim's boat — a forty-two-foot cabin cruiser, a twin-screw Matthews — to Brea Island. I had no idea what I'd find there, but I had a very strong desire to take a look.

"Anything you want me to do?" I asked Jim.

"No . . . well, yeah, there is one thing. Some of the Laguna Paradise people are probably wondering if I'm going to keep the development open today. After what happened last night."

"You going to close down for a while?"

"No. There's a chance somebody wants me to do exactly that — not that it makes much sense, but none of this does yet. If anybody does hope what happened to Aaron is going to slow down Laguna Paradise, I'm damned if it'll work. Anyway, if you want to you can call Wally and the girls and the rest, tell them nothing's changed. They're to go to Laguna today, as usual."

"Sure."

"I'd do it myself, Shell, but I've got to go downtown and complete the funeral arrangements."

"No trouble." He gave me the numbers to call and I jotted them down. "I'll be back here and ready to go by nine," I said. "And, Jim, take care."

The police had impounded the Smith & Wesson I'd used to poke holes in Mickey M. last night, but we'd arranged for Jim to carry another gun, a .38 revolver. I added, "Carry that heater with you."

"I'm way ahead of you."

We hung up and I made the calls, reaching everyone except Eve and Laurie, who didn't answer my ring. Of course, I didn't let the phone ring very long when I called Laurie, since that made it necessary for me to call in person. I hung up and drove speedily to the Claymore.

I went inside and stopped at the cigarette stand on the lobby's left, near the bank of elevators. While I was peeling off the clever little cellophane strip, I noticed a big chubby guy buying cigarettes. It was the middle-aged Santa Claus character I'd seen talking to Eve last night.

He opened the pack, withdrew a filter cigarette advertised as having the most "sanitary, safe, and effective" filter on the market, which allegedly soaked up 90% of the nicotine, 95% of the tars, and presumably 99% of the smoke. Chubby stuck the cigarette into a metal filter, which he then inserted with great care into his mouth. He got the thing lighted, and I wondered if he could taste anything. It seemed a hell of a lot of trouble to go to when he'd get so little out of it.

He noticed me eyeballing him, fascinated, and he was taken aback. Pale eyebrows went up a bit over bright blue eyes and he sort of cringed.

"Ah," I said, "hello, sir. Did you buy any Paradise lots last night?"

The brows went slowly down. I wasn't going to snatch his cigarette away, after all. He smiled, and it was a lovely smile. The way Santa would smile on Donder and Blitzen on Christmas Eve. "Yes," he said in a rather high but mellifluous voice, "yes, yes." It sounded as if he'd bought three lots. I was only one over that. "I purchased two," he said. "One is a splendid view lot, simply *splendid*. The other is small, but darling."

I thought: It's *darling*? A *lot*?

"I don't recall seeing you there, sir," he said. "Did we meet?"

"No. I was there with friends. I recognized you because I happened to see you talking to Eve last night."

"Eve?"

"Eve Angers, one of the models."

"Oh, of course. Of course. The salesgirls or whatever they are. One of them gave me quite a lot of information about lots."

It sounded a bit odd. But Eve had lots of lots, I remembered. He was saying, "A rather large creature, isn't that the one?" And I was thinking it was an odd way to describe Eve, but maybe not too far off the beam at that.

And that's not all I was thinking. The way my mind works, I could see three kings and hear Eve saying: *I'll zip you, Sweetie*. But I forced my thoughts away from her, and said, "You bought lots of lots — I mean, two lots, huh?"

"Yes, yes." He had it right this time. "I'm just delighted, especially with the view one. It's a perfect dream. You can see the blue Pacific, and the little waves frothing, frothing so whitely."

"Yeah, like Duz," I said, wondering what was with this character. Some people do talk like that, I suppose; and now I knew one who did. And he gave me the creeps. I said, "Toodle-oo," having caught something from him, and got away before I caught anything else.

Eve's room was 213 on the second floor; Laurie was in 420 two floors higher, and I saved Laurie for last. When I knocked briskly at 213 there was a short wait and then the door cracked open about three inches.

I could only see a little bit of her, but I figured it must be Eve. I could see a lot of black hair, beautifully waved with each glossy strand in place, the little bangs inky on her white forehead, and a cat-green eye with long lashes curling above it. But the eye looked a little different. Then I realized it hadn't been made up yet, and thus didn't have quite the sock it usually had. Besides which, just one eye and some forehead and hair don't have much sock anyway. I was thinking about that, and wondering why Eve was peeking so sneakily around the door at me, when she opened the door wide and not only answered the question but supplied lots of sock.

"Shell," she said smiling, "it's you. What a surprise."

"It's a surprise, all right," I said, but I was referring to Eve.

She was wearing a towel. At least a fuzzy white towel was wrapped around her torso, covering the vital thirty or forty per cent of her in a kind of haphazard fashion. It was a big towel, true; but Eve was a big girl. Some gals put on a towel and look merely like the week's wash, but not Eve. She looked like September Morn clutching a washrag.

"Come on in," she said.

"No . . . no, no." Despite the way I sounded I hadn't caught anything from Chubby after all. "I just came to deliver a message, Eve."

"Oh?"

I told her the Laguna Paradise personnel were to report as usual to the development and she said, "Well, I'd better get dressed."

"Yes, you'd better."

"I just got up. Just stepped out of the shower."

She was smiling at me, not holding that towel very cleverly — or maybe holding it *very* cleverly, now that I thought about it. She didn't have any makeup on, and looked a bit older, with slightly more obvious lines around her mouth and eyes, but not a hell of a lot older, and it was sure a young bath towel she was cleverly holding.

"I don't usually answer the door dressed like this," she said.

"That's good. I guess."

"Will you be at Laguna today, Shell?"

"I don't know for sure. Maybe this evening."

"Perhaps I'll see you there then?"

"Maybe." We smiled at each other and I said so long, turned and walked speedily down the hall as the door closed behind me.

I trotted up the stairs to the fourth floor and Laurie's room, rapped smartly, humming a little tune. I heard the sound of movement inside. "Who is it?" she called.

"Shell. Shell Scott."

She laughed. "Shell's enough," she said. "I remember your name. I remember you."

"And I remember *you*."

She opened the door. I was wrong. I hadn't remembered. Not all of it. Not the way it really was. This girl was new, every time you saw her.

"Hello, Laurie," I said.

"Hi. Come on in, Shell Scott."

I went in, told her I'd phoned a few minutes ago but hadn't reached her. It was true. Of course, I didn't tell her I'd only let the phone ring twice, then come here in a beeline, simply to see her.

"I thought I heard the phone ring. When I was in bed."

Laurie hadn't been out of it long. Her feet were nude, that is she was barefoot, and she wore a flowing white nightgown which cleverly concealed in a most revealing manner, and over the gown a matching and equally stimulating peignoir, and I would be crazy about peignoirs even if they were made of gunnysacks. Her hair was tangled and hadn't been put up yet, and there wasn't any makeup on her face. I'd caught both Eve and Laurie before they could apply the glamorizing touches of paint and powder, eye shadow and artful makeup; but Laurie didn't look any worse than usual. If anything, she looked better.

She went on, "I ran to the phone, but by the time I reached it there was just that buzz." She pretended to frown. "So it was you woke me up." She arched her back slightly and stretched a little, as if just now coming out of sleep.

"Ohh-hh," I said.

"What's the matter?"

"Nothing." I shook my head. "Laurie," I said briskly, "I came here to tell you . . . something. I'll have it in a minute. Ah, you're to go to work today."

"I wondered about that." Her face sobered. "Isn't it awful — "

"Right," I interrupted. No sense dwelling on it now.

"I — " she stopped, started over. "Except for that, until the phone rang last night, it was fun. Wasn't it?"

"Wonderful."

"I haven't laughed so much in a long time. And . . . well, it was fun."

"We'll have to do it again. Have a late supper, I mean. I've a trip to make today; but if I get back in time and we're both free for an hour — well, everybody has to eat. Maybe we could have dinner. . . ."

"I'd love to, Shell."

"In a restaurant. You know, a regular restaurant." I sounded like a sap. This Laurie made me a little uncomfortable. But I liked it. It was a very nice uncomfortable.

She said softly, "Anywhere you say."

Then there was silence. We just stood there, looked at each other, and there was silence.

And during it, I was thinking. Due to the nature of my work — and my own nature — to the place where I work — Hollywood — and, let's face it, due to plain, stupendous good luck, I have been around and involved with more lovely, shapely, exciting women than is good for a man. Although, really, that's probably good for a man. I have seen them in all shapes and sizes, colors and conditions, and I've learned one thing about them. One thing. That's all. And here it is, the total female-learning of Shell Scott:

It's good when a woman has the cast of feature and curve of body that men call lovely, or classic, sexy or sweet. That's good indeed. That's the form into which beauty flows. But the form itself isn't beauty. Beauty is that which flows. It's something inside, something which shapes the feature, lights the eye, warms the heart and lips. Take the same woman, alive and laughing, quietly asleep, cold and dead. Same face and form, nothing changes — except whatever it is that flows.

Call it electricity, spirit, personality, zip, zing, magnetism, fire — you name it. That's what beauty is, what it really is. And that's what Laurie had. In abundance, pressed down and overflowing. Probably other women possessed features as delightful as hers, eyes as bright and lips as warm, breasts as beautifully molded, waist as trim and slim, hips as provocative and legs as fine — but Laurie had whatever makes it work. She had the flow, the zip, the zing. Even with her hair a mess, without makeup to color her face, Laurie had it.

"What are you thinking?" She smiled.

"Why?"

"You had such an . . . oh, I don't know. Such a nice look on your face. What were you thinking?"

"I don't know the words to tell you, Laurie. But I'll try sometime."

"When?"

"When . . . when the time's right."

She laughed. "My, you sound serious."

I shook my head. "Don't I, though? Well, I didn't have any breakfast, and the sound you thought was distant thunder — "

"Oh, don't say it."

"Yeah, well, I'd better run. Just wanted to tell you about Laguna. Jim asked me to let everybody know."

I went to the door, and out.

Eight

Back at the Spartan, waiting for Jim to show up, I phoned the police and learned that no one had been ticketed for transporting a stiff in an auto, and no dead bodies had been found cluttering up the local landscape. But I got all the info I could on the late Mickey M., because I felt pretty sure I knew why he'd been snatched last night. With no corpse available, there could be no identification of the hoodlum — and thus no link to whoever had sent Mickey M. out on last night's job.

Of course, I did know who the gunman was. But the man who'd employed Mickey couldn't know I'd recognized the little hoodlum, nor could he know about Mickey's pinched chops on the time-lapse film Jim had shot.

The knowledge didn't do me much good, though, because the police didn't have anything that wasn't already in my head. Police records showed that Mickey M. — full name Michael M. Grauschtunger — had last been picked up for questioning in L. A. five years ago, and released. That was about the time I'd run into the guy, and the law had nothing on him since.

I'd brushed against Mickey when he'd been one of the youthful hoods growing into manhood in the gang headed by Lou the Greek. Lou wasn't actually a Greek; whatever his nationality, he was one-quarter slob, one-quarter ape, one-quarter sly brainy thief, and at least three-quarters sonofabitch. Lou had started his life of crime early, as a cat burglar — he stole cats — then graduated from reformatories to petty larceny and muggings, and finally gambling, the narcotics racket, and extortion. He had been sent to stir about five years back, and as far as I knew was still in San Quentin. The rest of his gang, including Mickey M., had scattered, and there'd been no official record of their movements since then. The police records did jog my memory about the other men chummy with Lou and Mickey M. in those days. I remembered Anthony Cini, known as Ants; the other three had been heavies named Blount, Fisheye, and Sneezer.

I pushed all that out of my head and picked up the phone to call a man named Ralph Merle, formerly a CPA and now an attorney who had dug up technical info and dope from official records for me half a dozen times in the past. I filled him in, told him I wanted everything he could get on Brea Island, its history and record of ownership, and all the info he could dig up about Handi-Foods, Inc., or whatever the factory was on the island. Ralph told me he'd get whatever he could by seven tonight, and keep on the job tomorrow if I needed more.

The chimes bonged and Jim Paradise was at the door. We climbed into my Cad and took off for Newport Beach.

Brea Island was forty miles off the coast, but about fifty miles in a straight line from the harbor at Newport, and Jim pushed his speedy twin-screw Matthews all the way. A little after one P.M. Jim pointed and said, "There it is, Shell. Brea. Maybe, in time, Paradise Island."

It had been a pleasant cruise to this point. For the first hour and more we'd been able to look back at the smoky pall of thin slop hanging over the coast, and free of smog for the first time in months our lungs must have been bewildered. Out here the world was fresh and new. The air was crisp, it was a bright sunny afternoon, and the horizon was a sharp, clean line. No haze obstructed our view of Brea Island, rising well out of the sea, four or five miles distant.

We'd been sprawled on the forward deck, the cruiser on automatic pilot, and now Jim went up on the flying bridge and took over the controls himself. He swung to port, steering south, away from the inhabited end of the island, not purposely to avoid being seen coming ashore — probably the boat had already been noticed — but to head for an inlet leading to a small calm bay where a crude dock had been built. In another half hour we were tying up at the dock.

There wasn't much on the island. Most of the land was covered with a profusion of low gray-green bushes, and some deep green shrubs bearing clusters of small pink flowers were scattered among angular rocks and low mounds and hills of earth. Jim and I walked around for half an hour or so while he enthusiastically pointed out spots where a hotel could be built, a small beach, the area where he imagined a nine-hole golf course.

Now, though, there was only one structure on this part of the island, a small shack like an old-west cowboy's bunkhouse, maybe fifteen feet wide and twice that in length. It sat in the middle of a wide flat area of land which obviously had been leveled with earth-moving equipment; the soil was loose and rich-looking, darker than the drier, undisturbed ground around it.

"Looks like good land," Jim said, "once it's worked and planted. Bring in a little topsoil and fertilizer, and plant some tropicals, a few palms, some ground cover, and you wouldn't recognize the place. That's what Aaron was going to do here, only . . . he never got to finish."

This seemed like a peculiar place to plant palms and tropicals, I thought. The island was only two or three square miles in area, I guessed, and this spot was a long way from the areas Jim had designated for the projected hotel, golf course, and so on, which were close to the sea.

I mentioned that to Jim and he said, "This wasn't to be permanent, Shell, just a sort of testing ground. We intended to bring in a lot of plants and palms and try them out, see if they'd grow well. Aaron thought we might even manage to transplant some coconut palms, the kind that're all over Hawaii. Experts claim they won't grow on the California coast, but we thought they might do O.K. here. If they did, we figured we'd put in a hundred or so near the hotel and along the beach. Make it a real — " he smiled, " — Paradise Island."

It was clear that developing this island some day was the real McCoy for Jim, the big dream — but I wondered if it had meant the same thing to Aaron. Jim trusted Aaron's motives a lot more than I did. Of course, Aaron hadn't been my brother. And because of that, knowing his background, I couldn't help wondering, just a little, if Aaron might have been planning some new kind of complicated con game. Maybe I was being unduly cynical and unjust; but I had known a hell of a lot more con men than Jim had, and not one of them had any more conscience than you could stuff in your ear.

"The building looks like a bunkhouse," I said.

"That's what it is." Jim walked toward it, saying, "I told you Aaron spent a lot of time out here, had a few men working with him for a while. They'd stay here several days in a row — had to, or they'd have spent all their time cruising back and forth from the mainland — so they built a place to sleep and cook."

It made sense, but I hadn't seen signs of any work elsewhere on this southern half of the island, and this area — not even planted yet — didn't seem like a very dynamic accomplishment. So I said, "Is that all they got done? Just building a bunkhouse and clearing off the land here?"

Jim gave me an odd look, frowning slightly, "For one thing they surveyed the whole damned island. That had to be done before we could decide on the best spots for a hotel and the rest of it, know where heavy rains would run off. . . . Why?"

"Just full of sappy questions," I said. Maybe I was just getting sour. In my business that's an occupational hazard — which I usually try to avoid. So I dropped the sappy questions and tried to look on the bright side of everything.

Jim led the way into the bunkhouse and we looked around. There wasn't much to see. It was a small, almost square room, with a couple of tables and a few wooden chairs, an iron woodburning stove, and along one wall a row of six bunks covered with dirty, greasy, oil-stained sheets and blankets. The whole place was about the filthiest dump I'd ever seen.

"Tidy, weren't they?" I said to Jim.

He grinned, apparently having gotten over his slight irritation. "No showers for tidiness. For that matter, no water on this part of the island, except the ocean. Let's hope they brought along lots of ice-blue Secret."

"They should have sprayed the joint with it." Something was puzzling me. I looked around. And then I got more puzzled. "Jim," I said, "doesn't this place seem a little small to you?"

"Well, they didn't need much room, Shell — "

"That's not what I mean. From the outside I thought this shack was maybe twice as long as wide. But it isn't; the room's nearly square."

Jim craned his head around. "Does seem peculiar, now you mention it."

I glanced at my watch. It was two-forty in the afternoon. "I'd better get over to that food factory," I said. "Or whatever it is."

"Want me to go along?"

"I'd just as soon we weren't both there at the same time — until I know more about it." I paused. "By the way, have you still got that .38?"

He nodded, patting his hip pocket, and said, "I'll meet you here, then. O.K.?"

I told him that was fine, and stepped out of the bunk-house.

The land sloped upward to a hill several hundred yards away that blocked my view of the north end of the island, but I headed in that direction, feeling good, enjoying the bright sun and air that had real oxygen in it. On top of the gently rolling hill were two huge wooden tanks, which I presumed were reservoirs Jim had mentioned, holding rain water and water pumped from the wells which had been drilled somewhere around here, gravity feed supplying the factory.

When I reached the hill's crest I could see below me several cultivated acres, green with low plants, and near them a long wooden building, apparently a shelter for some of the workers, a place for them to rest and sleep. Beyond all that, at the sea's edge, was the factory itself. The sight of it surprised me.

I guess I'd expected to see something like the crude bunkhouse I'd just left, but this was a huge flat building covering a good acre or more, freshly painted, a double row of clean glass windows facing the sea and mainland, the direction from which Jim and I had come. Plumes of steam issued from two vents at the far end of the building, and I could hear some kind of machinery clanking.

Four men stood near an open door in the building's front, all of them looking in my direction. When I reached them they simply stared at me silently, faces blank. They were pretty blank faces to begin with, and they certainly had no glad expressions of welcome on them now. All four men were dressed in gray-striped white coveralls and wore cloth-billed white caps on their heads.

"Hello, gentlemen," I said. "The boss around?"

"The who?" The man who'd spoken was a tall thin beanpole with bloodshot eyes and a scraggly mustache.

"The boss, the manager. Or owner — whoever's in charge of this . . ." I looked over the door at a sign, "Handi-Foods, Incorporated," and beneath the name a trademark picture of crossed spoons on a triangular white background.

The beanpole said, "What do you want with him?"

Something in the way he said it scraped me a little. "That's what I hope to tell him," I said.

He scratched his scraggly mustache, shrugged narrow shoulders, and said, "Come on in."

He ushered me into a roomy, pleasantly furnished office. It was empty, but my escort went out through another door and left me alone. I glanced around. There was a leather couch against one wall, opposite the door a wide brown desk with a padded leather swivel chair behind it. On the desk was a triangular name plate bearing the name, "Louis H. Grecian," and several colored brochures.

I picked up one of the brochures. It was advertising copy, and with a growing feeling of revulsion I noted that it sang the virtues of a food for infants with a brand name ghastly to contemplate: "Da Da Baby Foods." It was actually named "Da Da," and there were several varieties — strained spinach, mashed okra, green-bean, mush, various fruity concoctions. They all seemed pretty fruity to me, and for a brief moment I contemplated the advertising mind, imagined a dozen grown men sitting around a conference table, listening intently while one of them said, "Da Da. *Da* Da? Da *Da?*" But I contemplated the inspiring picture for only one brief moment, because I heard somebody behind me and turned around.

Just about filling the doorway was a wide, slope-shouldered character with hair peeping from the open neck of his shirt, gobs of hair on his head, hair on the back of his hands. He even had hirsute ears and plenty of hair in his nostrils. He was a very hairy fellow, this Louis H. Grecian.

I should have guessed, I suppose, when I saw the name plate on his desk. "Well," I said, "if it isn't Lou the Greek."

"What in the crud are *you* doing here?" he said, and he seemed truly amazed. Lou talked like that; he had a mind like an outhouse and a mouth like a spittoon. The criminal, the individual immersed in crime and violence, often speaks in language filled with foul imagery, its emphasis on the sexual and excretory functions. Lou was no exception. About every fourth word was unmentionable, and therefore need not be mentioned.

"I was about to ask *you* that, Lou," I said.

He repeated his question, shaking his head back and forth as if there were something in it that rattled.

I was a bit rattled myself, so I said, "Well, I'd like to look over your Da . . . uh, your baby-food factory, Lou."

He said several unmentionables, the gist of them being that I could look over his factory when the devil strummed a harp. Clearly he was not glad to see me.

The last time he'd seen me Lou had been handcuffed to a policeman, just before starting the scenic route to San Francisco, San Rafael, and then San Quentin, where the scenic route ended. I hadn't personally stuck him, but I'd been indirectly involved in the calamity which befell him. I had gotten the goods on a small-time pusher who had been selling marijuana to high school kids and heroin to the graduates. To the kids, that is, who graduated from joints to the hard stuff.

There it ended for me, but the police Narcotics Division pulled several items of info from the small-time pusher, items which included the intelligence that he'd been getting his decks of H from Lou the Greek. So, in due time, Lou had been put away in the slough. He blamed me, at least in part, for his misfortune. Of course, he blamed everybody — police, "square" citizens, society, everybody — but I was included. I knew he'd been called Greasy Louey as a kid, and later became Lou the Greek; but, oddly enough, until now I hadn't known his real name was Louis H. Grecian.

"I didn't know you'd been sprung, Lou," I said. "Are you still pushing junk?"

It just popped out, and all of a sudden I wished it would pop back in. Lou's face became suffused with what appeared to be very sour blood, and he jammed his teeth together, and pulled rubbery lips apart until muscles bulged unpleasantly in his cheeks, and hairs wiggled all over him. But that wasn't the worst of it. The worst was what started going on in my head when I said "pushing junk," and I got a very chill and queasy sensation, as if somebody had dipped my spine in cold cooking fat. Suddenly all I wanted was to be out of here and far away. There was a chance I could manage it, too; a fat chance.

My fat mouth and I were not now in the teeming metropolis, not in Los Angeles or Hollywood. We were stuck on an isolated island. Moreover, it seemed extremely likely that it had been Louis H. Grecian who sent his old-time associate, Mickey M., to call on Jim Paradise last night . . . and Jim, too, was stuck on this island with me.

As if that wasn't enough, several other unpleasant things were also going on in my head, but even with all that mental activity there was a separate little piece of my brain working, telling me what was going to happen next.

And what was going to happen next was this: One of these baby-food manufacturers was going to kill me.

Nine

Lou the greek almost seemed to grow larger, standing there in the doorway, his face reddening and veins throbbing on his forehead.

He was big enough to begin with, but looked larger than he really was, perhaps because of the hair sticking out all over him. He was five-ten and 180 pounds, with long arms, and long thin hands and fingers. His voice was like Death's rattle, and he had coarse features, a broken, flattened-out nose, and skin like the leather of an old catcher's mitt, and it wouldn't have surprised me to learn that he had six toes on each foot. He was a hard-boiled customer, no doubt about it.

He said, "Why you blank, blank, unmentionable, jerky gahdamn blank," and I got ready to slam him one on the mouth. But then, surprisingly, Lou started calming down.

It was an obvious struggle, but after a few seconds of silence he said, "This ain't gettin' us nowhere." He snorted air out his nose. "You always did give me pains where I never even heard of pains bein' before, Scott. You're like all the rest of the law, ride a guy forever just because he took a fall once." He snorted again. "I'm legit now. You can see I'm legit now."

"Uh-huh. This is about as legitimate as you can get, isn't it, Lou? Frankly, I didn't expect to see *you* here. I merely dropped in to see the Handi-Foods manager, whoever he might be."

"The boys — some of my workmen — seen the boat. You come out alone, huh?"

It was as subtle as getting kicked by a horse. "No," I said, "not alone. But there's nobody here but us Marines." I smiled, hoping he thought I meant an entire division. "And the boat," I added pleasantly. "You know, with engines, and two-way radio, and life preservers and such. And the two-way radio," I said again, in case he'd missed it the first time, "which is a sort of life preserver."

"Yeah." He paused. "Well, what'd you want to talk to anybody here for?"

I said, "You've heard about the possibility that the south half of the island will be developed?"

He nodded.

"I'm interested in the development," I went on. "Came out to take a look at the site. As long as I'm here I figured I'd check and make sure there weren't any objections from the Handi-Foods people — from you people, that is."

"There's objections."

"You object? What for?"

"Not me — this isn't my plant. I just run it for Lorimer."

"Horace Lorimer?" I asked. "He's been trying to buy the island, hasn't he?"

"Not that I know of. You'd have to ask him, but he ain't here today. He owns the plant, I just manage it, keep the boys, the workmen, in line."

"So what's the objection?"

Lou scratched the gob of hair at his throat. "For one thing, he don't want a mess of builders and machinery, and then tourists and kids, cats and dogs and no telling what-all tromping around, maybe getting into his vegetables. Besides, he's going to need more land — the right kind of land — so he can grow more spinach and beans and stuff for the canning."

I waved a hand in the direction of the already planted acreage I'd noticed. "Seems plenty more land out there," I said. "On this half of the island. He's got a lease, hasn't he?"

"Sure, but the best land's on the other end. For what he wants, anyway. He grows his spinach and tomatoes and all that organical — you know what that is, organical?"

"Without fertilizers?"

"That's only part of it. You don't use no chemical fertilizers, you use only natural stuff instead, like crushed rocks, and decomposed plants and leaves that's natural, like Nature does it in real life. But also you don't spray the plants with poison sprays like DDT and chlordane and dieldrin and those toxic poisons, see?"

Was this Greasy Louey talking? I could hardly believe my ears — especially as he really did seem to know what he was talking about. For example, poisons are sure toxic.

He went on, "Doing it like this, you get vegetables and fruits which are a lot healthier. They look better and taste better, and got more vitamins in them besides. In addition to which they're so healthy the bugs can't chew on them, so you don't need to spray much if any — which keeps any poison from being on the stuff which is going to be eaten up by the little infants."

For a while I couldn't say a word, trying to digest the indigestible. Finally, with real interest, I asked, "Lou, what in hell has come over you? The last time I saw you — "

"That was then, Scott. I've turned over a whole new leaf. I told you, I'm *legitimate*." He snorted. "Why won't you guys ever give an ex-con the benefit of a doubt?"

"Where did you come up with all that dialogue about organic planting and such?"

"Well, I — " He stopped, glowered at me, and said, "While in stir, I was the gardener. I grew all kinds of junk, everything from peonies to lobelia, carrots to potatoes."

"*You* did this?"

"It's a fact. I read in the library all about organical farming and gardening, and how all of us is being poisoned and killed slowly to death with poisons we eat. And drink. And smell, like smog."

"You can say that again."

"Planting them things in the earth, then watching little sprouts come up where there wasn't nothing before, I found — " He cut it off, then said, "Well, it made me feel peaceful and all."

I got the impression he'd started to say, "I found peace," and it gave me a very queer feeling for a moment. I would almost have walked over to him and started shaking his hand — except that I remembered last night, remembered Mickey M., remembered Aaron Paradise in a bloody bed.

So I said, "By the way, Lou, I ran into Mickey M. last night."

"You what? What's a mickeyem?"

"Right now it's a dead man. Michael M., who was one of your boys a few years back."

"Oh, him. Sure, why didn't you say so? Hell, I don't have nothing to do with them guys no more. Haven't seen Mickey — he's a dead man? Since when?"

"Since last night."

"What happened to him?"

"He got shot."

"I'll be damned." Lou snorted. "Well, it was bound to happen."

I was puzzled. Lou was quite convincing. Almost completely convincing. Almost. I wasn't ready to swallow this new Lou the Greek whole, however. Not yet. I said, "Funny thing, the man Lorimer leases this part of the island from was killed last night, too."

"Yeah." He nodded. "I know. That's tough."

"How come you know about Aaron Paradise, but didn't know Mickey was dead, Lou?"

It shook him a little. Just enough so he missed the important part of the question. "It was in the papers, so Lorimer give me a call and mentioned about Paradise," he said. "Seeing as how it might affect business, him holding the lease and all. Naturally there wasn't no reason for him to mention Mickey, if he even knew about him."

"Uh-huh. You've got phones out here, forty miles from the mainland?"

"You mentioned it yourself, Scott, there's a thing like radiotelephone. Like ship to shore, you know?"

He smiled, and while he was feeling pleased I stuck him with the rest of it. "Sure. And how come you knew his name wasn't Adam Preston?"

"Huh?" He blinked, scratched the hair on his neck, then the hair on his head. "What you mean by that, Scott?"

"Practically everybody else knew him as Adam Preston. His real name was Aaron Paradise. Which, apparently, you already knew."

He chewed on his lips, bushy brows pulling down in a scowl. "That's what I said, huh? Well, I guess that's what Lorimer told me. I don't know who in hell either of the bums was. O.K., Scott? Or are you getting kind of big-mouthed?"

"Not me," I said genially, and had the feeling it was time to vacate the premises while I was still ambulatory. "Well, never mind all that," I said. "I've got to get back. See you, Lou."

He nodded, and I walked out.

Nobody stopped me, and that not only relieved me but surprised me more than a little. I kept glancing back, and could see Lou the Greek talking to two men. They looked in my direction. That didn't have to mean a thing. But something else might mean quite a lot.

I was looking toward Lou and the two men, and happened to glance to my right. A guy in the building, several feet down from the office, was eyeing me through a window. I got just a glimpse of him, but a glimpse was enough.

It was a face easy to remember — a round, fleshy face the color of mashed potatoes, with a lumpy, globular nose in its middle, sparse light hair on the head — the face of a guy called Ants. Anthony Cini, another of the boys who, like Mickey M., had been in Lou's old gang. "I don't have nothing to do with them guys no more," Lou had said.

Well, maybe. Maybe Ants Cini, too, now planted seeds in the ground, and found peace by watching green things growing.

In a pig's eye.

Ten

When i was hidden from anybody who might be watching from the factory I started running, veered right and went up the side of the low hill until I could look over its crest. From here the factory was about three hundred yards away — but two hundred yards away were a couple of chaps moving fairly rapidly in my direction. They weren't running — not yet — but they were walking like men in a big hurry.

I turned and ran some more. When I reached the bunk-house I yelled Jim's name and jumped inside. He wasn't there. I called his name again and heard him yell, "Out here, Shell," his voice a little muffled.

When I got outside and moved around the corner, I saw Jim. He'd pulled away a loose board, flush with the ground at the end of the bunkhouse, and was just crawling out. There was oil, or grease, on his hands and staining his trousers.

As he climbed out he was talking. "After you mentioned it, Shell, I noticed the bunkhouse *was* bigger outside than inside. There's a little room at this end, sealed off, no door or anything."

"The hell with that — "

"Looks like they were fixing up a giant can for this place, or a still," he said grinning. "Or else it's a Sputnik. Some kind of pipes under there, but they aren't connected to anything yet — "

"Jim, if you don't shut up, the next sound you hear may be guns going off."

"Guns? What in hell are you talking about?"

The men were in sight now. I'd made real speed getting here, but they were only two or three hundred yards away — and running, making pretty good speed themselves.

"I have just listened to a lot of jazz about gardening and pure baby foods," I said, "and maybe it's true. And maybe I was just supposed to think it was true. But those two — "

"Gardening and baby — "

"Listen to me, Jim. The guy who tried to kill you last night was Mickey M. Mickey M. used to work for Lou the Greek. The guy running that damned baby-food factory over there is Lou the Greek."

He nodded, listening intently now.

I pointed. "Those two guys may be bringing us some fresh cucumbers. But that's open to serious question, so you hightail it to the boat while I stall them."

"I'm not going to leave — "

"With you on the boat, where they can't get at you, it's not likely they'll try anything with me. Assuming they've anything unpleasant in mind." The two men were still coming toward us, but more slowly now. They were staggering, and not making a lot of headway, clearly in lousy condition. But they were too close to suit me.

I knew there was a flare gun complete with colored distress signals on the boat and I told Jim to cruise off shore near the factory and in twenty minutes start shooting off the flares in the direction of the factory, but not near enough to hit it; just near enough to excite lots and lots of interest.

He said, "Crazy," but spun around and ran toward the cruiser.

He had nearly a minute in which to sprint away before the two men reached me. I even had time to take a peek past that loose board at the end of the bunk-house. It was dark in there, but enough light came through cracks in the thin boards forming the walls so I could see a goofy conglomeration of pipes and valves rising six or eight feet above ground level, but not connected to anything at its top. It looked like a giant erector set designed for grown-up nuts; or maybe Jim had been right and it was a still, like for manufacturing triple Zombies.

"Crazy," I echoed Jim, then stood up and kicked the board loosely back into place as the sound of galloping feet reached my ears. I stepped away from the building as the two men staggered up, stopped a yard from me, and stood there, tottering and making wretched noises. One of them was the lanky beanpole. He pointed at the fleeing Jim and said, "He . . . Where's he . . . Oh-h." It took him another half-minute before he could say, "Where's he going? Wha — what's be . . . running for?"

"What were *you* guys running for?"

"Why, uh . . . We, uh . . . Uh . . ." He never did think of an answer. But he went on, "The boss, Lou, he says we should ask you and — " He looked toward Jim, a dwindling dot now about to climb aboard the Matthews. "You and, uh, your friend to come back to the office."

"Why?"

"Why? Well, he forgot something."

I said, very pleasantly, "Maybe he wanted to know for sure who was with me, and how many of us there were, and sent you to make certain nobody failed to respond to his kind invitation."

"Now, that don't make a bit of sense," the beanpole said.

"Maybe not. Well, let's go see what Lou wants."

Lou was seated behind his desk in the office this time. When the three of us came in he looked at us then past us, as if expecting somebody else. After looking a while, and frowning ferociously, he pulled his face into an expression approximating pleasant good-fellowship and said, "There you are."

"Here I am, Lou."

The beanpole said, "There was another guy with him, but he run to a boat."

"He's out there listening to the two-way radio," I said.

Lou kept his stiffly happy expression on and said, "Ah, that don't matter. I really wanted to see you, Scott."

Sure, and he grew peonies as a hobby. I said, "The boys tell me you forgot something, Lou."

"That's . . . right."

He looked stricken. He had forgotten what he'd forgotten. I tried to make it easy for him to remember, because that was the reason I'd come back here so peaceably. "Hell, Lou," I said sincerely, "I thought you wanted to apologize for blowing up when I asked a simple question."

"What question?" There was hope in his eyes.

"When I asked if I could look through the factory. Believe it or not, I've never been through a baby-food factory."

"Damned if that isn't it, Scott," he said jovially. "I shouldn't of blown up at you like that, and I realized it just the instant you was gone out of here. And I'd sure like to show you through the factory. Yes sir."

"You've got a heart of gold, Lou."

"Be with you in a shake." He got up from his desk and went into the next room, taking the two men with him. He came back without them and jawed with me for a minute — possibly, I thought, so his boys could do whatever he'd told them to do. Such as getting Ants Cini out of the way, or hiding the submachine guns. I looked at my watch. Just over five minutes left. When those flares went off, maybe nothing would happen; but possibly it would take a little attention off me. What I'd do then — if anything — I had no idea.

Then the tour started, Lou Grecian conducting it himself and the beanpole tagging along. The whole building — except for about a fifth of it at one end which contained Lou's office, a kitchen, and some other offices and storerooms — was one huge room devoted to the production of canned baby foods. I'd almost expected to find nothing here, but the place was crammed with complex machinery and cardboard cases of small cans packed four dozen to a case.

I stopped and picked a can out of one of the cases and looked at it, while Lou was explaining that "in them big vats over there" vegetables were stewed before being canned. The can I held had a picture of a healthy, rosy-cheeked baby on one side, and the crossed-spoons-on-white-triangle trademark on the other. I finally figured out that the white triangle was a diaper, and shuddered. The can was strained peas and carrots, and I put it back into the box.

Lou was pointing out some of the machinery and explaining how the empty cans were carried along on moving tracks, filled with the still-steaming mush, and efficiently sealed. It was all very impressive. I was convinced that canning really was done here, but there wasn't a piece of machinery in operation, and the three of us were the only people in the huge plant at the moment.

I said, "The joint is wild with activity, isn't it?"

"Hell, not now," he said. "Not on Sunday. There's only a stand-by crew here on weekends, rest of the boys go home Fridays on the company boat." He waved a hand toward the area where hundreds of cases were stacked. "You should of been here Friday when we finished canning this batch. We'll ship most of it out tomorrow."

"You really ship it out, Lou?"

He looked straight at me, and for a moment his eyes were hard, but then he got that good-fellowship look again and said, "He jokes. Always a joker." He stepped forward and picked up a sheaf of papers. "This shipment goes out to San Pedro tomorrow, Scott. Ordered by the M. W. Wilson chain. Here's the papers on it."

He showed them to me. Lou was really anxious to convince me. Or so it seemed. But the papers did show that about a hundred cases of Da Da Baby Foods, broken down into a dozen different kinds of vegetables and fruits, were going out on tomorrow's date to M. W. Wilson. And Wilson's was a widely known chain of supermarkets.

So they shipped baby foods. So what? It was a baby-food factory. Maybe I was nuts. The twenty minutes had passed, and probably Jim was shooting off his flares now. Again, so what? I hadn't seen anything of much interest to me.

Glancing around, I noticed two cases, filled with the little cans, separate from all the other cases. They were against the wall, under a table, one case on top of the other. The sight interested me mildly, and I walked toward them, saying, "What are those cases, Lou? Rejects?"

It was really only mild interest at that point. But as I stepped forward, the long beanpole on my left jerked as if stuck in the hind end with a sharp stick. Before I could take another step, he got in front of me.

Now my interest was no longer mild, so I managed, clumsily, to step on the guy's foot. "Hey!" he said.

"Sorry," I said, and managed to land on his foot again.

Lou said, "That's right. That's some rejects, like you said." He kept stealing my ideas. "Some of the cans get sort of crimped around wrong going through the line, and naturally we can't send those out."

"Naturally not."

It had been twenty-three minutes by now, and I decided Jim's flares hadn't caused any curiosity at all. Or else the old flare gun hadn't worked. But I had let hope die too soon. At that moment a man stuck his head in the door and shouted, "Boss! Boss!"

Lou looked around and screamed, "Quit yelling. What's eating you?" From his tone, something was eating Lou.

"There's a funny thing . . . A guy in a boat is shooting something at us. Flares — or rockets — or . . . something."

Lou swore and said to me, "What're you trying to pull, Scott?"

"Me?"

He let go with a few more choice expletives and started toward the door. Then he stopped and turned back toward us. I looked away at the silent machinery, so I don't know what kind of signals he gave to Beanpole, if any. But from the corner of my eye I saw Beanpole nod slightly. ·

Lou walked briskly out, slamming the door behind him. That left the lanky guy and me alone in here, so I took a step and managed to bounce on his foot again, bumping him a bit in the process.

"Listen, you lousy bastard," he said, and grabbed my right arm. So I swung my left and popped him. I got him a good one on the underside of his chin and he sailed away from me, landing on his back. He lay there silently, and I was moving as he landed.

I grabbed a can from the nearest case, which turned out to be filled with strained spinach, ran across the big room to the two cases beneath that table. I slid the top one to the floor and grabbed a can from the middle of the bottom case. This stuff was labeled "Mashed Bananas." Maybe that's why they were rejects. Who would eat mashed bananas? I dropped the spinach into the empty space in the banana case, hoisted the second case atop it again, and sprinted back to the spinach. When I dropped the banana can where the spinach had been, all appeared normal. I fumbled in my coat pocket, found a ballpoint pen, lifted the case and scratched a big "X" on its bottom, dropped the case and put the pen back into my pocket. Then I leaped back to stand over the still unconscious man — barely in time.

The door crashed open and Lou Grecian barged in yelling, "What in hell are you pulling, Scott?"

I was dancing around next to the fallen man, making belligerent noises. Grecian stopped next to me, looked down at the man on the floor, then at me, his features much as they'd been when I'd first seen him standing in the office doorway.

Then the anger faded a bit, and his eyes flicked around the big room. They seemed to linger overlong on the two cases by the wall, but I could have imagined that. "What happened here?" he said in a voice that could give tender ears hernias.

"This slob got big-mouthed and made a grab at me, so I had to lean on him a little, Lou."

Grecian didn't say another word until some cold water had been tossed on the unconscious man's face and he'd become conscious. He sat up, eyes not quite focused, and Lou put his face close to the shaken man's and said, "Scott here says you popped off at him, and took a grab at him. Just tell me clear and simple. Did you?"

"Well, he was tromping on — "

"Shut up. What I want to know is, did what he says happen, or is Scott lying?"

"Well . . . yeah, it happened. I called the lousy bastard a lousy bastard. And I guess I grabbed him but it was only he was tromping — "

"Ah, shut up." Lou was disgusted. He straightened up, walked forward a little, looking around, then came back to me. "What's with them flares?" he said.

"Flares?"

He uttered his favorite word, smacked his lips, and said, "Oh, hell, why in hell don't you get the hell out of here?"

"O.K., Lou. Isn't very exciting in here anyway."

He kept me in conversation in the office until one of the workmen, who had been in the plant briefly, came back in Lou, I thought, looked relieved. Just as I was ready to leave, a big guy stepped up behind me and started to pat me under the arms and along the legs.

I spun around and slammed the edge of my palm against his biceps, and was about to slam him again when Lou said, "Hold it, Scott. Easy, dammit."

I looked at him.

Lou said greasily, "You don't mind a little shake, do you?"

"Warn me first."

Lou nodded to the guy who'd started patting me. He was squeezing his arm. I said, "Just a minute. You must know I carry a gun, Lou, so don't get all excited." I took the Colt out, and lifted my arms so the guy could give me a quick shake, which he did, while I kept the .38 pointed at Lou.

Then I put the gun back in its clamshell holster and said to Lou, "What in hell you looking for? Carrots?"

"Union rule," he said, and his eyes were cold enough to frost his nose. He wanted to keep me here. That is the definite impression I got. Maybe I was wrong; but it was sure a strong impression.

Outside, I could see the Matthews a couple hundred yards off shore. I walked toward it, waving one arm and indicating that Jim was to go back toward the dock. On the far end of the island. Far away from gardener Lou the Greek. Nobody came after me. From there on out, it was easy. Jim pulled into the dock, I jumped aboard the cruiser, and we put-put-putted away.

Eleven

When I was sure we were free of the island and nobody was following us, I told Jim most of what had happened back there. Then I thought for a while about what I'd seen and heard in these last couple of hours. But I was also thinking about Laguna Paradise.

I knew the total value of improvements on that land when the development was completed and everything sold, would probably reach sixty million dollars, a good portion of which would be profit. I knew, too, that though a few of the people associated with Laguna Paradise had invested money and would share in the profits, the bulk of the investment and risk — and thus profit — would be Jim's.

Now I said to him, "Jim, with Aaron's death you fall heir to his interest in Laguna Paradise, don't you? And to Brea Island, for that matter?"

"I guess that's right. I hadn't thought much about it, Shell. But, yeah, I guess I do."

"Uh-huh. Next question. What if Mickey M. had hit you dead center last night? What then?"

"I don't get you."

"Who'd wind up with your interest in Laguna Paradise? Your money, estate? Who'd inherit?"

"Nobody."

"Come on, Jim. When anybody dies — "

"No kidding, Shell. Aaron and I were the only children, Mother died two years before Dad, neither of us has a wife, there are no living relatives. None."

"Well, somebody's got to . . ." I stopped.

Jim said, "When a citizen dies and there are no legal heirs, the estate escheats — all of his property and estate goes to the State. The State

69

makes sure it gets its gravy, either by taking it all, or at least grabbing estate and inheritance taxes." He shrugged. "Which is a very fat grab, by the way."

"Well, suppose somebody knew that and wanted to bid on Laguna Paradise, in case it went on auction — "

"Shell, the Laguna thing isn't worth a bent penny at the moment. Right now it's owned almost lock, stock, and barrel by the banks, the finance companies."

I thought about that for a minute, then went on, "O.K., back to the island now. I told you that Mickey M. worked for Lou the Greek, and Lou's in charge of that factory. They actually brew baby food out there, can it and ship it to various spots on the mainland. I'm convinced of that. But consider: this Lou is a hard-boiled hood; he hasn't been out of stir very long, but here he is running a factory making — I'm not kidding — Da Da Baby Food."

"Making *what*?"

"My reaction, exactly. Bear with me. Lou went to the sneezer for pushing narcotics. He now claims to be a reformed character, giddy with the joy of planting asparagus and such. O.K., maybe; but suppose he is a great big liar, and hasn't reformed a bit? Suppose he, instead, is planting H in cans of strained gooseberries, say?"

"H? You mean heroin?" Jim's eyebrows went way up over his blue-green eyes.

"Exactly."

"In cans of *baby food*?"

"Why not? Look, one of the toughest — and most dangerous — factors in the junk business is getting large quantities of junk from the major producing areas — Red China, Mexico, and so on — into the point of sale, the place where it's to be cut, sold, and used. Like the U.S.A. International hoods have spent a lot of sleepless nights figuring better, safer, more certain methods of transporting and delivering narcotics. It's not just important to them, it's vital. So junk has been carried by couriers; hidden in big brassieres on flat-chested babes, and in false bottoms of trunks and coffins and people. And one hell of a lot of other techniques that worked for a while and then went sour."

Jim was nodding. He ran a hand slowly through his black hair and said, "I'm getting the message."

"Sure. Look, I'm talking about the big leagues. If a little pusher in L. A. gets picked up, he loses a few decks, or at most a half ounce or so, of heroin. But when a big shipment, a kilo or two, gets grabbed — man, that's murder." I smiled slightly. "Figuratively speaking, that is. If it gets through, then it's murder literally. Anyway, the loss of big shipments means a loss of millions of dollars to the big-time punks. But suppose you could easily get the junk to a safe spot — an isolated island, say — and little packets containing an ounce or two of heroin were sealed into cans, in a separate run at the plant, maybe in the middle of some gooseberry soup . . ."

Jim was frowning. "Yeah, they could ship it openly, anywhere in the States. In the world, for that matter. And who would suspect narcotics in — what did you call it? Da Da?"

"Yes, ugh."

"Do you actually think that's what's going on out there?"

"Hell, I don't know. But judging by the charming Handi-Foods personnel, if I'd seen any poppies growing on the island I'd think they were raising their own opium, and somehow processing it into morphine and then heroin. Actually, it's just a wild guess, but maybe I'll know more tomorrow. There were a couple cases of gunk out there and either I'm a nitwit or there was something more than canned burps in them — judging by the reaction of those characters. Anyway, I managed to pull a switch with some cans set to be shipped ashore tomorrow." I grinned. "But probably they're producing delicious, organically grown baby foods for health food stores. When I'm wrong, I'm *really* wrong."

"In case you're not wrong . . . Do you suppose Aaron might have stumbled onto something like — " He stopped. "No. If he had, he would have said something to me about it."

"Well, you can bet your life on this: If the Handi-Foods setup is a front for smuggling narcotics, the boys who went to such pains and expense to set it up would kill several dozen guys before they'd let the racket be exposed."

"Probably. But it can't have anything to do with Aaron. Or his death. But . . . just supposing it did, why the try to kill me last night? I sure as hell never heard of that stupid baby food, much less anything about narcotics. So why me?"

I shook my head. I didn't know why. I let it all simmer, as we headed back into the smog.

After dropping Jim off at the development, I found a phone in Laguna Beach and called the Police Building in Los Angeles. I talked to Captain Feeney, head of the Narcotics Division, described the setup on Brea Island, told him of my suspicions, and explained about my slipping the can of mashed bananas into the spinach case. His men would check and determine if a shipment from Handi-Foods, Inc. really was going to the M.W. Wilson chain tomorrow, and if so would arrange for a "food inspector" to find and examine the case I'd marked when it arrived in San Pedro. It would be handled as a matter unconnected with a police investigation, to avoid stirring up the animals if I was right and to avoid embarrassment if I was wrong; and until the result of that check was known we would all sit tight.

From Feeney I learned that Grecian had been sent to Q on the narcotics rap in late 1957 and got out in early 1959; he hadn't served much time. But narcotics murderers have a pretty soft touch in California — especially since the U. S. Supreme Court voided California State law by ruling that addicts mustn't be sent to the can for addiction. That wouldn't be nice at all, so California mustn't do it, said the Warren Court in effect; it would be "cruel and unusual punishment." The presumption was that the hypes deliberately sticking needles into their arms — and usually pushing dope, stealing, mugging, boosting, prostituting, pimping, or even murdering in order to get their "medicine" — were "sick" and not really guilty of any crime.

The next step, I presumed, would be a ruling that rapists and murderers and safecrackers were sick rather than criminal, and instead of being imprisoned should be sent to Sunnybrook Farm. Eventually, I supposed, it would be a criminal offense to be a law-abiding citizen.

It was interesting to note, however, that Grecian was in San Quentin in 1959; and at that time, so was Aaron Paradise.

I asked Feeney if he would arrange to have Aaron's body checked for evidence of narcotics addiction; he would, and I hung up.

Next I phoned Ralph Merle. He was still in his office, and after gabbing a bit and commenting that he'd been reading about me in the newspapers, he got down to business.

"Here's the dope," he said. "Brea Island, owned by the Spanish until — you want all this?"

I grinned. Ralph was a guy who believed if a thing was worth doing it was worth overdoing, and he had probably traced the island back to the time of Columbus. "Just the last few thousand years or so, O.K.?"

"Start in 1948, then. Purchased in March of that year by Drake Patterson for $35,000. He owned it until he sold it to Horace H. Lorimer in August 1955 for $20,000."

"Wait a shake. He sold it to Lorimer? Of Handi-Foods, Inc.?"

"The same, manufacturer of Da Da Baby Foods. Not bad stuff, by the way."

"You mean you've heard of — I hate to say it — Da Da Baby Foods?"

"Sure. Fed it to my own kids for a while. It's good stuff. Why?"

"You can really buy it in the stores? It's not just some fly-by-night outfit?"

"On the contrary. It's been on the market for several years, and it's good. Sold in some supermarkets here on the coast, and in most health-food stores — carefully selected and processed for nutritive value, that sort of thing."

"I'll be damned," I said. "In health-food stores, huh? O.K., go on."

"Lorimer, owner of Handi-Foods, Inc., built his first plant on Figueroa here in Los Angeles in February of 1956. In November of '57 he sold out and built a factory on Brea Island — which he'd bought from Patterson more than two years before. Nine months ago, in September 1961, he sold the island to Aaron Paradise."

"Huh? He sold it to Aaron Paradise? But . . ." I stopped. "But Lorimer's the guy who was trying to buy it . . ." I stopped again.

Ralph continued, "Anyway, Lorimer sold the island to Paradise for $420,000 — "

I interrupted again. "For *how* much?"

"For $420,000."

I whistled. Where in hell had Aaron Paradise gotten $420,000? Plus another $50,000 or so which Jim had told me he'd had when he showed up in Southern California. The total of 470,000 clams was a lot of chowder for anybody to have, but especially a man only a year out of prison. Of course, Aaron was — at least had been — a con man. Something wiggled in thought, but then stopped wiggling.

I said, "This is goofy. And how come the island sold for $20,000 in '55, and only six years later brought $420,000?"

"Don't ask me. I'm just telling you what's on the record."

"Uh-huh. About this Lorimer. I take it he's a legitimate businessman."

"Oh, yes — well, yes and no. As I said, the product's a good one, the company doesn't make a lot of profit but seems in good shape. Lorimer, too — except that he had some income-tax trouble recently." I heard him chuckle. "As who doesn't?"

"Yeah, funny. What kind of tax trouble?"

"Just a second. I've got the dope here somewhere." I heard the rustle of papers. Then Ralph grunted and went on, "Government sued him for back taxes for the years fifty-seven, -eight, and -nine. Suit was initiated just a year ago this month and settled last December. He wasn't prosecuted for fraud, but he paid up, $360,000 including penalties. In fact, the government released its lien on his property and put a claim into escrow — the escrow on the sale of Brea Island — for the amount of their lien against Lorimer."

"Whatever that means."

"It means the proceeds from the sale were enough to satisfy the government's claim." Ralph was silent for a moment. "Then Paradise leased the north half of Brea Island to Handi-Foods, Inc., the corporation to pay him rent of $50,000 a year for the twenty year life of the lease."

"Hold it. Is that legal?"

"Not only legal, but sale and leaseback is quite common — and smart, under today's tax setup."

"The lease was so Lorimer would have the use of the land his factory was on, huh?"

"It was to Handi-Foods, Inc., from Aaron Paradise, and I quote, '. . . only for the purpose of agricultural, storage, warehousing, manufacturing, and all other uses incidental to the manufacture of, Handi-Foods products.'"

"And this resulted in Handi-Foods' agreement to pay Aaron Paradise $50,000 a year?"

"That's right."

"Interesting. How about this Patterson? Anything fishy about him?"

"I should say not. He's Drake Patterson, designer and builder of the Patterson boats, sailboats, cabin cruisers. You must have heard of them."

I had heard of them, seen several of the boats at Newport. The "Drake" cabin cruisers were world famous.

I said, "Have you got anything on a man named Louis H. Grecian?"

I heard the rustle of papers again. "General manager of Handi-Foods, Inc. Since . . . December of 1959. That's all I have on him, just the name."

"That's O.K. I've probably got all I need on him." I smiled and added, "He's an ex-gardener."

Ralph, with his usual efficiency, had dug up Patterson's and Lorimer's addresses for me. Patterson lived on nearby Lido Isle, which I could pass on the way back to Los Angeles, so I headed over there.

Drake Patterson was an old man now, seventy or more, I guessed, but he impressed me as being a vigorous old character, and he had an outdoors look about him. He was a big florid, white-haired man, the flesh a little loose on what once must have been a powerful frame, but he still looked as if he could handle any other seventy-year-old who might give him a hard time. Patterson was bluff and hearty, open and frank in his speech. I liked him on sight.

He lived on the top floor of a luxurious new cooperative-apartment building on Lido Isle, adjacent to Newport, and we were sitting on the small deck off the living room of his apartment. It was nearly eight P.M. now, not quite dark, and from here we could see the full length of the lovely harbor, hundreds of boats in the water, lights coming on along the shore.

I'd told him I was a private investigator but had only hinted at the information I was after. He'd made a bourbon and water for me, and was sipping brandy in a shot glass. "Brea Island," he said. "All right, young man, what do you want to know about it?"

"I understand you owned the island for a while, then sold it a few years back. Is that right?"

"Yes. Bought it in, let's see, forty-eight, I think it was. Meant to build a home there for my wife and me. I like the sea, the solitude out there, and an island's the next best thing to a boat. The home was really for my wife, but I kept putting off getting started, for one reason or another. Busy making money, keeping the company going, figured there was plenty of time. I did finally get the plans started, but before they were finished, Mary died."

He paused, then added, "Mary was my wife. After that there didn't seem much point to, well, to any of it. I turned most of the business

75

over to my associates, started getting rid of things — property mostly. Among the property was Brea Island. That went in fifty-five I think it was. Don't remember who bought it, offhand."

"Horace Lorimer?"

He nodded. "That sounds right."

"Then you sold the island to Lorimer for $20,000?"

He started to answer, then stopped. "What difference does it make what he paid for it?"

"Well, the island's changed hands since then, and less than a year ago it sold for $420,000. It seems strange that in six years it would bring twenty times what it originally cost."

"That's a pretty good profit," Patterson said, "but it isn't unprecedented in land speculation. It's a matter of supply and demand, Mr. Scott. Nothing has any intrinsic dollar value you know; it's how badly somebody else wants what you've got, how much of their labor or production, represented by dollars, they're willing to trade for it. Supply and demand always works, if allowed to, and it's always basically fair in the long run." He sipped his brandy. "Of course it's allowed to work less and less these days." He was quiet for several seconds, then in the near darkness I could see his head turn toward me. "Is the price paid of any real importance to you?"

"I don't know. It might be. The man who bought the island from Lorimer was killed last night." I didn't explain about my meeting with Lou Grecian but indicated there might be a connection between the murder and the victim's ownership of the island.

Patterson finished his brandy, laced his hands around one knee. "Well, I'll tell you something, Mr. Scott," he said. "I doubt that there was anything really wrong with the transaction. Certainly I didn't do anything I felt was immoral. But there was one . . . peculiar circumstance. I was asking $80,000 for the land. Mr. Lorimer actually paid me $100,000. But there was one condition — he insisted that I represent the sale, and show the price on the sale papers, as only $20,000."

I blinked. "Why in blazes would he do that?"

"I don't know. But he offered $20,000 more than I was asking, and I couldn't see that I was doing anything really reprehensible. He talked a good deal about his wife, with some malice, as I recall, and I remember getting the impression he might have a good deal of money she didn't know about. If you understand what I mean."

"Trying to conceal assets in case of an alimony grab?"

"Either that, or perhaps he simply didn't want his wife to know he had that kind of money to spend for an island — or for anything else." He chuckled softly. "I suppose there are husbands who do that sort of thing."

"It's been rumored."

"Yes. Well, I agreed to Lorimer's terms. His was the only offer I'd had, and at that time, all I wanted was to clear up everything, get the slate clean." He paused, looked at me again. "Speaking of a clean slate . . . While the sale was listed at $20,000, and I did receive $100,000, I entered that additional $80,000 on my tax return that year as income from the sale of real property — I actually made a profit of $65,000 over what I'd paid for the island. So the appropriate bureau of our burgeoning Socialist state received its just share of my profit. Or, if you think at all as I do, its unjust share."

"I think exactly as you do." I finished my drink, lit a cigarette. "I can't figure Lorimer, though," I said.

Neither could Mr. Patterson.

I was back in Hollywood and walking into the Standish, a very-upper-bracket apartment hotel on Wilshire Boulevard, by ten-thirty P.M. And once again I was going to a building's top floor, because Horace Lorimer lived in one of the two penthouse suites.

I didn't phone or announce myself, just went up in the elevator, found Lorimer's door, and pressed the mother-of-pearl button alongside it.

One chime rang softly inside, and in a few seconds the door opened. Horace Lorimer looked out at me, and I said, "Well, I'll be damned."

Twelve

The guy in the doorway was Chubby, my modern Santa Claus, the chap who'd bought two lots at Laguna Paradise. He had a filter cigarette in the metal filter, and the filter stuck in his mouth, and he looked at me as if pure nicotine were squirting onto his tongue.

I said again, "Well, I'll be damned," and he said, "Goodness gracious!" We weren't the same sort at all.

Then he said, "Good evening, Mr., er . . . I don't believe I know your name, sir, do I?"

"It's Shell Scott. You're Mr. Lorimer? Horace Lorimer?"

"Yes; I am, Mr. Scott. Yes. Did — did you want to see me?"

"If you don't mind. I would like to talk to you for a few minutes."

"Please come in."

He stood aside and I walked into the living room of a penthouse suite that looked like — well, like a penthouse suite. The carpet was thick lavender, a low white divan slanted into the room on my left, two ornately carved black wood chairs were near the right wall. Farther away on my right was a gleaming black piano, keys exposed as if ready to bite. Lavender draperies were open before a wall almost entirely glass, beyond which was a sparkling view of the city's lights. Large oil paintings brightened two walls, and there were several pieces of sculpture in the room, a bust of some bearded philosopher, a beautifully fashioned female nude with upstretched arms on a pedestal. On a small table at the left of the white divan stood a foot-high nude figure of a young man, looking down at a baby in his left arm and holding a bunch of grapes over his head in his right hand. At least I'd seen that one somewhere before, even if I couldn't remember what it was called. Sometimes I feel I lack culture; but usually I don't think about it.

We sat on the white divan and I said, "Mr. Lorimer, I'm a private investigator. Right now I'm checking on the ownership of Brea Island." That stuck him. For one reason or another, it stuck him. He said, "Brea Island? What did you want to know?"

"You sold it several months ago, didn't you?"

"Why, yes, I did." He pursed his lips and frowned, looking as fierce as a canary with a cat. "However, sir, I fail to comprehend what business that is of yours."

"The man you sold it to got knocked off last night. Killed. Murdered."

"Yes, I saw that in the press. But I repeat, I fail to see what business — "

"I suppose I am being nosey. It's really a matter for the police."

That stuck him, too. He shut his eyes in a kind of wince, held them shut for a count of three, then opened them wide. He looked like a kid caught with his hand in the cookie jar. This guy was guilty as hell of *something*. Maybe stealing cookies.

I went on, "The police may want to talk to you, once they check into all of the deceased's affairs, but I thought I'd try to get here first."

"Yes . . . well, I — naturally have nothing to conceal. That is, no objections to answering your questions."

"Fine. Nine months ago you sold Brea Island to Aaron Paradise. For $420,000. Right?"

"That is correct."

"Do you have any idea where he got that kind of money?"

"No. He deposited certified checks for that amount in escrow. I didn't ask him how he earned the money."

"Why did he want the island?"

"He didn't say."

"How did you meet him?"

"Last summer he came to the island, while I was there at my factory, and approached me about selling him the island. I was, well, in need of capital, and after a few days of discussion we settled on a price. That's all."

"Uh-huh. You mentioned your factory — you own Handi-Foods, Inc., don't you?"

"Yes. In a way. Well, yes."

"And you're the manufacturer of Da Da Baby Foods?"

"Yes." He was smiling at last. "Yes, Da Da is — my baby." He simpered so cutely I almost threw up. I'll say one thing for Horace Lorimer, he looked a hell of a lot more like a baby-food manufacturer than the creeps I'd seen at the factory. He looked as if he ate the stuff three or four times a day.

"Tell me about it," I said. "If you will. I mean, how you started, built up the business and so on."

"You're really interested?"

"And how."

"Well, I've always loved puttering around in a kitchen." That figured. "And I love children — I have none of my own."

"You're still married, Mr. Lorimer?"

"Yes. But Gerda isn't with me at the moment, she's in San Francisco. We have an apartment there, too, and spend quite a lot of time in that lovely city. She, especially, spends a lot of time there." I wondered if I'd detected a note of pique; he sounded miffed.

"My mother left me a bit of money," he went on. "Well, one can never trace precisely how these things happen to one, why one chooses a certain vocation rather than another. But I do recall being with friends when they were feeding their two children something out of a can. It was a horrid concoction. I tasted it myself, and believe me, Mr. Scott, it was simply *vile*."

"I'll bet."

He sighed and let his hands flutter. "I began thinking then of the possibility that I might produce a product not only healthful but tasty. I've long been a student of nutrition. I believe it was then I truly made up my mind, though I must have been thinking about it for some time — for some time it must have been subconsciously *stewing*." He simpered again.

"I began studying, investigating, and about a year later bought property in Los Angeles and built the first little factory." He went on to tell me of starting his factory in Los Angeles, "nursing" the business along for several ticklish months, to use his phrase, and then being delighted when sales soared.

"The business grew beyond my fondest expectations," he went on. "I found I simply *had* to expand, but the land on which I'd built my little factory was atrociously expensive — there wasn't any more available in that area, anyway. I fear I had failed to consider that factor in the beginning." He smiled sweetly. "We all make mistakes, don't we?"

"Ain't it the truth."

"Well, I was between the horns of a dilemma. But, oddly enough, there was a way out, even though at first I didn't realize it. A year or two earlier I had purchased Brea Island, intending it as a site for a summer home. I vaguely considered transferring my base of operations there, but at first it seemed ridiculous — you know, a baby-food factory on an island. Out in the ocean."

"I confess, it struck me as an odd place to build a factory."

"Ah, but further consideration made the prospect more and more appealing to me, Mr. Scott. You see, I'd purchased the land very cheaply, almost for a song. And I *already* owned it, there would be *no* capital outlay whatsoever. Moreover, I owned a small yacht which, with minor redesigning, would be ideal for shipping my product to the mainland. I wouldn't even have to pay anyone else for transporting my Da Da."

I shuddered. But, then, every tune I heard that gah-danmed name I shuddered. I said, "Sounds like a dandy setup, Mr. Lorimer. And you say you bought the island for a song. About how many notes in that song?"

"Eh?"

"Would you mind telling me how much you paid for the island?"

"Only $20,000 for the whole thing."

"That's not what Patterson said."

"Patterson? That's the gentleman from whom I purchased Brea Island."

"Right. And he says you paid him one hundred thousand clams."

"Clams? I presume you mean dollars. *Well,*" he said huffily, "clams or dollars, I paid twenty thousand."

"You're sure of that?"

"Of *course* I'm sure. Shouldn't *I* now what I paid for it? Why in the world would Mr. Patterson say I paid more? If he did say that," Lorimer added significantly, looking daggers at me.

"He said it. O.K., let that ride for now. You might tell me why you've got those slobs working for you on the island."

"Slobs?"

"Muggs, hoods, cons. Lou the Greek for one."

"Lou the Greek?"

"Louis H. Grecian. Your general manager. Tell me you don't know him."

"Oh, Mr. Grecian. I know him. Indeed I do know him. He's terrible, revolting man."

"I'll go along with that. But if he's so terrible, revolting, why did you hire him as your manager?"

"I . . . didn't exactly hire him."

The story unfolded. All had gone along well with the factory on the island, sales increased, everything was sweetness and light and mashed carrots and vitamin-filled beans until about the middle of 1959. Then Lorimer had begun having labor troubles. He'd been happily, successfully non-union, actually paying well over comparable union scale, then some "rather awesome" looking characters had come to the island and proceeded to unionize his plant. Soon the employees asked for a raise, and Lorimer granted it; then came demands for fringe benefits, pensions, overtime, additional employees, and he acceded to those demands. But that wasn't enough — it never is. It turned out that the man with apparently total power over the unionized employees — they did what he told them to or he arranged to "pull their cards" and they couldn't work at all — was: guess. Yep, Louis H. Grecian.

To make the long but not unusual — except for its ending — story short, Grecian forced Lorimer to take him on as general manager in December of 1959, and hire several of his hand-picked friends. All this, of course, in the name of labor, peace and "the rights of the working man."

Lorimer, his face a bit twisted, said, "It was the most terrifying display of union power. I was completely helpless. I could get no assistance from the national union, not even from the courts. It seemed I was some kind of monster, depriving the union man of his just standard of living, his rights, something like that. I, oh, I became almost incapable of work. I became ill. This may sound foolish to you, Mr. Scott, but to me it was the end of a dream."

"It doesn't sound foolish to me, Mr. Lorimer," I said.

The Handi-Foods situation was a little unusual in that the man with obvious control of the union local — Louis Grecian — had no official, on-the-record position *in* the local. So Lou the Greek, ex-con, virtually controlled the management end of the business while at the same time largely directing the union with which that management had to deal. I shook my head in frustration not unmixed with admiration; what a marvelous setup it was — for a crook.

Lorimer was saying, "Actually, that's why I sold my interest in the island. I had wonderful plans for massive expansion, plans to raise fruits and vegetables organically all over the island, pick them when they were most tender and delicious, produce a truly superior food for the babies. It's rich, virgin soil, too, never farmed, never poisoned by fertilizers or toxic sprays."

So that's where Grecian got the idea, I thought. "You told Lou Grecian all this, I suppose?"

"Yes, for hours — at first. Before he proved himself to be so impossible."

"You've been trying to buy the island back, though, haven't you?"

His eyes got wide again. "No. Certainly not."

"Oh? You're sure of that?"

"Of course I'm sure."

That's not what Jim Paradise had told me. So one of them was lying. And I was sure it wasn't Jim. But I let it ride, lit a cigarette and added casually, "By the way, you had some trouble with the tax boys, didn't you?"

He blinked the bright blue eyes. "Well. Where in the world did you learn about that?"

"I picked it up. You came out of it O.K., though, didn't you?"

"Oh, yes. Yes, indeed." He laughed bitterly. "I survived the ordeal splendidly — except for surrendering $360,000 of my money. It was either that or go to prison. In your business, Mr. Scott, that would be called extortion, wouldn't it?"

"Hell, I'm not arguing, Mr. Lorimer. At least you're not in the can — in prison."

He pursed his lips. "Laws can be passed to make *anything* a crime. Do you realize, Mr. Scott, that 'a heavy progressive, or graduated, income tax' is one of the cardinal points of the *Communist Manifesto*?"

"Sure. Point two, between 'Abolition of property in land' and 'Abolition of all right of inheritance.' But, since we're stuck with it, Mr. Lorimer, what was the beef against you?"

He glared at me. "That, really, is none of your business. But I'll tell you. I deducted several items from my gross income, which were not allowable — or so the government agents alleged. Among them were costs of my yacht, which they claimed I used largely for pleasure, part of its cost, and so on. At any rate, I was informed I couldn't deduct those and other items, and thus had to surrender a good deal of money."

He was right; it was none of my business. So I wondered why he'd told me. Lorimer sounded off some more about the fact that extortion by individuals was a penal offense but by government bureaus it was called taxation or "wealth distribution," the effect of a steeply progressive income tax being to inhibit most the most productive individuals, thus bringing all men down to a common level — of dependence on those who confiscated the taxes. I let him get it off his chest, partly because I wanted him to get the steam out, and partly because it was true, and I agreed with him.

But it was also true that Horace Lorimer's story seemed to have a large number of holes in it. So I said, "Thanks very much, Mr. Lorimer. That should just about do it." And I stood up.

He looked relieved, almost happy, Santa again, smiling at the reindeer. While he was feeling so jolly I went on, "There is one thing — the way this looks on the record. Without the explanation you've just given me, I mean."

"Oh? What's that?"

"Well," I said, almost apologetically, "You owned Brea Island and sold it to Aaron Paradise, then for some reason — so, at least, it has been alleged — began trying to buy it back. And last night Aaron Paradise was murdered. Also a hoodlum named Michael M. tried to kill his brother, Jim Paradise. Very likely Michael M. is the man who did both jobs — and he was probably working for Louis Grecian." I shrugged. "You see how it might look to the police."

"Police?" It was almost a squeak.

I went on, "Since Grecian works for you as general manager of Handi-Foods and you're the whole cheese of Handi-Foods, and since you allegedly want to buy Brea Island, it might look as if you — not only Lou Grecian, but you as well — might have had something to do with the trouble last night. The shooting, the killing — "

"No! Good heavens, kill — no!"

"It might look that way to the police, Mr. Lorimer." I paused. "But if you tell them the same facts you've told me, that will probably satisfy them." He had thought I was all through with him, and now I was shaking him up again. His usually pink face was pale, and he kept running his tongue over his lower lip.

I went on, "Naturally I'll have to tell them about our talk."

"Tell . . . the police?"

"Of course."

"But you mustn't."

"I'm sorry, Mr. Lorimer. But I'm a licensed investi — "

"You mustn't!"

I turned my back on him, stepped toward the door.

"Wait!" he said.

And it was a queer thing — something in his voice, some kind of telepathic transmission of emotion from his mind to my own, or maybe just the keyed-up state I'd reached waiting for whatever it was I knew he was almost ready to say — but I got a cold, scratchy feeling along the middle of my back, as if somebody were running a sharp icicle over my spine. I had the sudden, perhaps totally irrational, conviction that Horace Lorimer might be preparing to shoot me in the back of the head.

I stopped, glanced over my shoulder. Lorimer sat quietly, hands resting on his knees, staring fixedly at me. His face was still pale, but he wasn't aiming guns or even icicles at me, just his eyes. His frightened eyes. Fright? And of what, I wondered, would Lorimer be frightened?

"Wait," he said again, softly this time.

He seemed to sag, all soft and puddly once more, the Da Da man again.

All right," he said. "I'll tell you the rest of it. I'll tell you all of it."

Thirteen

Lorimer was quiet for almost a minute, then he said, "I have a request to make of you first, Mr. Scott. If, when I finish, you agree that I've done nothing *truly* reprehensible, not committed any terrible crime, you won't report to the police what I'm going to tell you."

I thought about it. Finally I told him, "If it's something I feel I can overlook, I'll sit on it for a while. In any case, I'll tell you before I leave this room what I mean to do about it, if anything."

He nodded.

"That is, if you convince me you had nothing to do with what happened to Aaron and Jim Paradise."

"I had nothing to do with any of that. I swear it. I read of it in the press, but that's all I know. However, Mr. Scott, I didn't tell you the truth about the sale of Brea Island to Aaron Paradise. I never sold it to him at all."

"Wait a minute, I had official records checked — "

"Of course it's listed in official records as a legitimate transaction. It *was* a legal transaction. You'll understand in a moment." He sighed, rubbed his hands together. "I've explained what Mr. Grecian did with me, with the factory. Well, with union gouging and coercion crushing me on one side, and the monstrous and confiscatory tax structure hammering me from the other, I was caught between intolerable pressures — as many other small, and large, businesses are today, Mr. Scott."

"Amen."

"In the hope of salvaging something from the wreckage, for some years I entered on my individual income tax returns deductions which were perhaps, well, questionable. Business and entertainment expenses, the yacht expenses I mentioned, that sort of thing, which enabled me to lessen the tax I was forced to pay, keep *some* of my money for myself. You understand?"

"So far."

"Well, as you apparently know, a year ago the government instituted suit against me for non-payment of taxes in 1957, '58, and '59. They alleged I owed them $360,000 in back taxes and penalties for those three years." Lorimer sighed. Perspiration was moist on his forehead and upper lip. "That presented me with another, rather peculiar dilemma. You see, I actually had enough money to settle the claim — but according to the income shown on my tax returns, and the other deductions and expenses I had listed since 1959, I should *not* have had that much money left. Is this clear to you, Mr. Scott?"

"I think so." What I guessed he was saying was that he had continued to "cheat" on his income taxes and wound up with quite a bit of undeclared income; but if he used it to settle the tax lien against him, the government might then ask him to explain where he got *that* money — and maybe sue him for some of it, too.

He was going on, "I could pay the allegedly owed tax — and face possible further prosecution because I had the money to pay it. Or I could claim inability to pay, in which case the U. S. Government would seize and sell my assets, including Handi-Foods and the island, to settle my — well, my legal debt. But then Mr. Paradise came to see me and suggested a solution."

"When was this?"

"Nearly a year ago. Shortly after the government instituted its suit against me."

"Did you know each other before then?"

"No, we'd never met. I hadn't ever heard of him."

"Did Aaron know Lou Grecian?"

"No." Lorimer shook his head, then added, "Or if he did neither of them ever mentioned knowing the other." He paused. "Incidentally, that's how I met Miss Angers. It was through Mr. Paradise — she was with him on a few of the occasions when we later met."

"Who?"

"Miss Angers — Eve. You asked me about her this morning, and I pretended I didn't know her. I shouldn't have, but you caught me by surprise, and I was trying to keep all this a secret — about my dealings with Mr. Paradise." He waggled his head. "I had no idea it would ever come up again."

"Uh-huh. Let's get back to Aaron. What was this solution you say he suggested?"

"He seemed to know a good deal about me, and was aware of the government's tax suit. During the conversation he learned what I've told you, that I did in fact have enough money to pay the government's claim but couldn't explain possession of that sizable sum. Mr. Paradise's solution was basically quite simple. I would give him $420,000 of my own money. Then I would 'sell' Brea Island to him for $420,000, thus receiving my money back from him. I could then claim I had received the money — with which I could satisfy the government's suit — from sale of the island."

I blinked. "Wait a minute. Let's see if I've got this straight. No money changed hands, right? That is, Aaron didn't kick in with any money of his own."

He nodded.

"But you did legally transfer title to the island to Aaron Paradise."

He nodded again.

"And you merely dug into the sock, your sock, and pulled out $420,000 of your *own* money, which you had accumulated through tax evasion — "

"I prefer to call it tax avoidance, Mr. Scott," he said a bit stiffly. He was caught in the cookie jar again.

I sat there and chewed on what he'd told me, and got it largely digested, though there was still a puzzling lump somewhere in the middle of it. I said, "O.K., Aaron put the idea up to you. What happened?"

"We went ahead with the transaction. Since there was a general lien on all my property, it was not possible for me to dispose of any part of it without permission. In tax cases, you understand, a citizen is adjudged guilty until proven innocent, rather than — "

"Yeah. So?"

"I met with Internal Revenue agents, with officials of the U. S. Government. I proposed to sell Brea Island, which had a tax basis to me of $20,000, for $420,000, if the government would release the lien on my property. This was agreed to, providing that the United States could place a claim in the escrow and from its proceeds be satisfied for all taxes, penalties, and interest. This, of course, was precisely what we desired, and was therefore agreeable to all parties concerned."

I sat quietly for a while, letting it all slop around in my head. Then I said, "O.K. I follow you to here. The tax boys got their money, and Aaron wound up with title to Brea Island. But then you leased part of the island back from Aaron, didn't you? And paid him rent on the land?"

He blinked the bright blue eyes rapidly. "Good grief. You know almost as much about my business as I do, don't you?"

I smiled. "That's *my* business, Mr. Lorimer."

His face was shiny with perspiration, and he seemed to get paler. "Yes, I suppose so. . . . I suppose it is." He licked his lips and went on, "I was coming to that. In fact, that's a vital part of my explanation to you." He paused. "Actually, Mr. Paradise suggested this, too, and it truly is an excellent idea. You see, if I sold the land outright I could take no deduction from corporation profit, no part of the $420,000 whatsoever. But by cancelling the lease I personally held on the land, selling the land to Mr. Paradise, and then having the corporation — Handi-Foods, Inc. — lease half of it from him and pay him rent, one hundred percent of that rent could be deducted from corporation prof-its. Which means the rent of $50,000 a year could be deducted and escape the fifty-two percent corporation tax."

"Then the corporation actually was going to pay Aaron $50,000 a year?"

"Well, ah, no. You see, that was part of his agreement. Nothing would be paid to him, really. But, ah, the corporation could nonethe-less deduct $50,000 a year from corporate profits."

"In addition to simply sticking fifty G's into that old sock, hey?" I waggled my head about. This guy was beginning to strike me as some kind of crooked genius. Maybe he wasn't a genius, but he was sure as hell some kind of crooked. I almost had to admire him, though, if for no other reason than his ability to remember what the hell he'd been up to.

"It sounds beautiful," I said. "If a bit ugly. But with that lovely setup, why were you trying to buy back the island from Aaron?"

He shook his head. "I was not attempting to buy the island from him. I repeat, Mr. Scott, you have apparently been misinformed. The purpose of transferring title to Mr. Paradise was, first, to enable me to settle the government's suit, and, second, to gain the obvious tax advantage a sale-and-leaseback arrangement would provide me and Handi-Foods — and that advantage accrued only so long as I did not own, but was paying rent on, Brea Island. It would therefore be folly for me to take title to the island again."

I nodded. "Makes sense. Just one things bugs me."

"Bugs?"

"Bothers me. What did Aaron get out of all this?"

"For providing the idea, and cooperating in helping me out of my dilemma, he asked — and I gave him — $50,000. I simply handed him that amount in addition to the $420,000."

"You did give him $50,000 then? Eight or nine months ago?"

"Yes."

So that explained where Aaron had gotten the fifty G's he'd had when he met brother Jim again. It explained, too, how he'd been able to pay an additional $420,000 for Brea Island. He hadn't paid it; Lorimer had.

Then another thought struck me. "This rental deal you had with Aaron — that, I assume, was an oral agreement between the two of you?"

"Naturally. We could hardly, ah, draw up a binding contract to that effect."

"Hardly. So you're stuck now, aren't you? I mean, with Aaron dead, that oral agreement doesn't mean a thing."

"Precisely. You're quite astute, Mr. Scott. And that is why I've confessed this . . . peccadillo to you."

Peccadillo. It sounded like a little armored lizard. But I was now getting the drift of Lorimer's conversation. "I think I understand. If Aaron hadn't been killed, you would actually have paid him no rent, but could continue to deduct $50,000 a year from corporate profits."

"Precisely. Later we planned to lease the other half of the island for, say, an additional $35,000 or $40,000, ah, rent. So it was of the utmost importance to me that Mr. Paradise remain alive. With his death — well, for me it is almost catastrophic. I may lose the island entirely, and I have already lost the $50,000 I paid Mr. Paradise. I will probably actually have to *pay* the rent of $50,000 a year. Not to mention the taxes, the taxes. . . ." He looked like a man having his leg broken. "You can see that, more than anyone else in the world, I wanted Mr. Paradise to stay alive."

He'd overstated the point, I thought, but it did make sense that be would have wanted Aaron alive and cooperating. It certainly seemed unlikely that Lorimer would have wanted him killed.

I said as much, and Lorimer asked if I was going to withhold from the police what he'd told me. I told him I'd sit on it for a day or two, until I had more information. The answer failed to satisfy him, but I didn't give a hoot if it did or not. I wasn't completely satisfied, myself.

But this time, at least, when I got up, I went out.

I had plenty to think about. Besides all the rest, this added one more bright facet to Aaron's character. For sure, he had still had a larcenous streak in him.

From a pay phone on Wilshire Boulevard I called the Police Building in L.A. and asked Narcotics if the body of Aaron Paradise had been checked, as I'd requested, for evidence of addiction. It had been — and the report was negative. I hung up, scowling, more disappointed than I should have been. Which shows the folly of jumping to conclusions. I'd half convinced myself Aaron had been hooked.

At home, I phoned Ralph Merle again, and asked him to check first thing in the morning on Drake Patterson's 1955 income tax returns, to determine if that extra $80,000 had indeed been reported. Then I called Jim Paradise.

"Shell here, Jim. Any more trouble?"

"No, all's quiet. But I've been damned careful. How's it going?"

"O.K. I've picked up some more info." There seemed little point, on the night before Aaron's funeral, in hitting Jim with further evidence that his brother had not been exactly the all-American boy, but I did say, "Jim, didn't you tell me a man named Horace Lorimer was trying to buy the island from Aaron?"

"That's right."

"Wonder if we're talking about the same guy."

He described Horace, from fat to pink face to filter cigarettes, and I said, "Same guy, all right. Was last Sunday the only time you met him?"

"No, I'd seen him several times before. With Aaron most of those times, I guess. What about Lorimer?"

"He just got through telling me he wasn't interested in buying the island, that he hadn't approached anybody about buying Brea."

"Then he's lying. I wonder why."

"Yeah, so do I. Here's another thing. Did you know he's the guy who sold Brea to Aaron in the first place?"

"The hell. No, it's news to me. If he wants it back, why did he sell it in the first place?"

"It was — some kind of a tax deal. I'll fill you in on the rest tomorrow, Jim. Unless you want me to buzz out tonight."

"No, you don't need — wait a shake. You could do me a favor."

"Name it."

"I left Laguna early, so I didn't bring in the records of the day's sales, as of closing tonight. I saw Eve before I left and asked her to bring them in — we'll be closed down tomorrow. If you feel like it, you could get the records from her and bring them out here."

"Sure. I'm supposed to see Laurie tonight at the Claymore, anyway."

"I was going to run into town and pick them up, but I'd just as soon stay here. I've . . . had a drink or two." He sounded tired. "There's the funeral and all tomorrow, you know. Beiglen Mortuary at one P.M., incidentally. Then graveside services at Greenmont. Were you planning to attend the funeral, Shell?"

I loathe funerals. If I had my way, the only funeral I'd attend would be my own. In fact, if I *really* had my way, I wouldn't even attend that one. But I said, "It's up to you, Jim. Maybe you'd rather I didn't — "

"Frankly, I'd like for you to be there, Shell. That is, if you don't mind."

"I'll be there. O.K., see you later."

We hung up, and I pushed from my mind thoughts of corpses and death, and headed for the Claymore, thinking of life — and Laurie.

Fourteen

"Hi, Shell Scott," Laurie said. Her smile lit up her face, and the room, and quite a lot of me.

"You don't have to call me Shell Scott any more," I said. "We're friends now, aren't we?"

"Fresh. Come on in."

I went in. She said, "Are you free for the evening, or are you still investigating and cogitating and skulking or whatever you do."

"Still skulking, I'm afraid." I told her I had to run out to Jim's, so if we had our late supper it would be pretty late.

"Let's take rain checks, then," she said pleasantly. "I'll forgive you this once. Anyway, I got hungry and had a sandwich. For all I knew, you'd forgotten our date."

"Funny." Laurie wasn't dressed to go out. She wore a white dressing gown and low-heeled shoes. But her hair was done in an intricate hair-do, her makeup was on, and except for the outfit she was ready to go.

We walked to the divan and sat down, while she told me Eve had brought in the papers for Jim, so I could get them from her. "But there isn't any terrible, terrible hurry, is there?"

"There is no terrible, terrible hurry."

Laurie had apparently been reading, and a book lay open, face down on the arm of the divan. I picked it up and said, "What are you reading, Proust?"

She laughed, possibly recalling Jim's comment at Laguna Paradise when we'd all been discussing that first party. "Whoever he is. Did he write about chess?"

"Beats the hell out of me." The book was a collection of Emerson's *Essays*. "Ah, Ralph Waldo," I said. "There was a man. Should be required reading for the New Frontiersmen. And the Supreme Court. And other fat — "

"You don't know," she said lightly. "You're the physical type, you don't read books, do you?"

"Sure, like crazy." She was teasing me, I guessed. So I said loftily, "Why, last year I read *two* books."

She smiled. "Name one."

"That's easy. I, it was, uh . . . It was all about a fellow named Tarzan — there's a physical type for you. It was called *Tarzan's Secret Treasure*. I read that one, all right."

"Prove it. What was Tarzan's secret treasure?"

"Jane."

She laughed. "You're pretty smart after all."

"I take after Tarzan."

We kept yakking away and wound up discussing Emerson's essays, believe it or not. "Self-Reliance," "Compensation," "The Over-Soul," Laurie knew them all — even better than I did. And after a while it occurred to me that this was not exactly the kind of thing I usually talk about when alone with a gorgeous tomato. Not exactly the kind of thing I ever talk about, if you want the truth.

And it was time to be on my way. So I said, "Ah, me. It's not that I want to go. But go I must."

"It's been fun."

"Fun indeed."

"Call me tomorrow?"

"Sure."

"You still owe me a dinner."

"A pleasurable debt, which I anticipate paying with wild — anticipation."

I started to get up, but she was very close, looking at my face, her lips slightly parted.

It seemed like the most natural thing in the world. It *was* the most natural thing in the world. She came into my arms without a sound, without hesitation, easily, wonderfully. And her lips were wonderful, sweetly burning, fire and honey.

It was a kiss to make monks say the hell with the monastery; to make hermits bomb their caves and start shaving. And I am not a monk, I am not a hermit. I am something else entirely; and this gal had enough electricity in her to turn on all the lights in Carson City, Nevada. She sure turned me on, anyway.

I said, "Woman, you just burned off all my insulation, short-circuited my generator, blew my fuses — "

"What are you talking about, Shell?"

"Don't you know?"

"Well, I've got an idea."

"That's the idea."

I hauled in a big hunk of air. "Yes, you understand, all right." I hauled in another hunk. "That's what we need in this old world, more understanding and . . . and . . ."

"Sympathy?"

"Not exactly."

"Shell, why don't you stop talking and kiss me again?"

"Why not?" I cried. And that was the one that did it.

Well, I have done my share of kissing — and maybe even a little more — and I have been around at moments of oscillatory invention staggering to fevered imaginations. But this thing opened up whole new dimensions of osculation. It gave mouths a new meaning, and justified having lips in the first place, and it was . . . well, it was lots of fun.

I knew I ought to get out of there. I knew I wasn't going to make it. I didn't.

I walked out of the hotel, into the cool air, and was half a block down the street before I realized my Cad was parked in the opposite direction. When I turned around, I remembered I hadn't done what I'd come to the hotel to do in the first place. I had done something else. But I still didn't have those papers for Jim Paradise.

I looked at my watch. It was a little after two A.M., but I trotted up to the Claymore's second floor, anyway. Light showed under the door of 213, so I figured Eve was still up. I started to knock, and the door opened, and I almost tapped pretty Eve on the nose.

She let out a little squeal.

"Sorry, Eve. I'd just started to knock."

"My, you startled me," she said, the pale green eyes wide. "I was just leaving."

She was fully dressed, wearing a dark gray suit and high-heeled gray shoes, carrying a big black-leather bag closed by leather drawstrings at its top. Her glossy hair was neatly in place, with those little-girl curls inky against the smooth white of her forehead. The pastel makeup was expertly applied, oriental eyes accented, orange-red mouth moist and gleaming.

She was a very striking sight, and to some she would have been feminine pulchritude, beauty, and simmering sex. But nothing stirred. Not in me.

"Lucky I caught you," I said. "Jim asked me to drop by and pick up the records on today's sales at Laguna Paradise. I almost, uh, forgot."

"What a coincidence. That's where I'm going now. He was going to call, but he never did."

"I know. He mentioned it to me quite a while earlier. I should have given you a ring, I guess."

"I can run them out, Shell. You needn't bother."

For a moment I wondered if Jim might not be much more pleased to see the voluptuously-fashioned Eve instead of me, but then I remembered the funeral tomorrow. I said, "That's all right. Eve. I'll take them. Jim's probably feeling pretty low tonight."

"Of course." She smiled slowly. "Well, I didn't need to get all dressed then, did I?" She had a way, all right. The words came out like asterisks, or the dots at the end of jazzy paragraphs in books.

"You might as well come in. . . ." Eve said.

"O.K. Just for a little."

We went into the room. Eve waved toward a little portable bar on wheels in one corner and said, "Like a drink?"

"Yes, I would. Thanks."

"Help yourself. I'll be right back."

She went into an adjacent room. Just before she closed the door I got a glimpse of a bed in there. Her bedroom. She'd better not come out dressed in something "more comfortable," I thought; she'd better not. And I proceeded to mix myself a healthy belt of bourbon and water.

But Eve came into the living room again after only a minute or two. She had, fortunately, merely removed the gray jacket of her suit. She was still carrying her bag, from which she extracted a sheaf of papers. "Here's the information Jim wanted, Shell" She said, "Mix me one of those, too, will you?"

"Sure." I looked at the bottles on the little bar. "Bourbon? Brandy? Scotch?"

"Make it a brandy," she said, "with a little soda. Anything but a Gintini, right?"

I grinned. "Those were pretty caustic, weren't they?"

"Like Drano in a — oops. Yes, caustic."

I spotted a phone on a table, asked Eve if I could use it, and called Jim. Fortunately he was still up, and undismayed by my tardiness. I told him I'd be out in half an hour or so, then joined Eve where she sat on the couch.

We swallowed some of our drinks, then I asked her, "You know a guy named Horace Lorimer, don't you, Eve?"

"He's a fat man, tall, red-faced?"

"That's him. Looks a little like Santa Claus."

She laughed. "He *does*. I never thought of it, but he does. Without whiskers." She sipped her drink. "He bought two lots. Might even buy more — he's loaded."

"You met him a while before he bought the lots, didn't you?"

She looked at me, raising the penciled brows questioningly. "Yes. Nearly a year ago, I guess. Why?"

"What do you know about him?"

"Not much. He makes some kind of cra — oops. Some kind of junk. Baby food, I think. Must sell a lot of it, he sure spends the money." She rolled her eyes toward the ceiling, then slanted them across at me, smiling. "Not on me, though. He's not my type."

That, I thought, might rank as the understatement of the twentieth century. "How'd you meet him?"

"Last summer, I was with Aaron — " She stopped. "I never mentioned knowing Aaron — or Adam as he called himself — did I?"

"No, but I already knew you'd gone out with him a few times."

"How in the world did you know?"

"I had a talk with Lorimer earlier tonight. He mentioned it."

"Not that it matters, really. It's just that — well, the idea that I'd go to that party with Jim and you, the same night his brother was killed, and the way the party was . . . it wouldn't seem right to some." She smiled slightly. "Especially the way that party developed. It just didn't seem like the kind of thing a girl ought to talk about."

She went on to say she'd met Aaron at a Hollywood party shortly after he arrived in Los Angeles. She was already modeling then, and a guest at the party. They'd met there, hit it off pretty well — she would have caught Aaron's eye like a hook — and had gone out together a few times. "But he couldn't be content with one woman," she said. "Flit from flower to flower, sampling the different honeys, that was Aaron."

The rest of what she could tell me, the parts she knew, matched all that Lorimer had told me. "They had some kind of business deal on," Eve said, "but they never told me what it was all about."

They wouldn't have, I thought. But at least what Eve told me corresponded with what Lorimer, who impressed me as a pretty tricky talker, had said. So I dropped it, finished my highball.

"Like another one, Shell?" Eve said.

"No, that one will bold me. Thanks."

"Not even a Gintini?" She laughed. I shook my head and she went on, "Speaking of those gin concoctions of Jim's, that really was quite a party, wasn't it? Too bad it had to end."

"Especially the way it did."

"Yes. But — let's not dwell on that, Shell. Let's think of the . . . happy things."

"Sure."

"And I really did have a marvelous time. . . . That wonderful dinner, and all the rest of it. I'll confess something." She looked straight at me, arms crossed and hands hugging her shoulders, those cat-green eyes narrowed, slanting, fixed directly on my own eyes. "The way we talked before at Laguna and all, it was just — just kicks. I didn't think I'd actually play strip poker."

I swallowed.

"Even when Jim was shuffling the cards. Not even then."

"I remember. You, uh, needed a little encouragement."

"And got it." She breathed a little more heavily, nostrils flaring. "But once I'd started, once I'd thought: Why not? — it was fun." She dropped her arms to her sides, leaned against the cushion behind her and threw her head back.

Her words led me back to that suspenseful moment when Eve had decided to join wholeheartedly in the game. Or maybe wholeheartedly isn't quite the word. Any more than game is. And there appeared in my mind a vivid picture of Eve sitting on the white carpet, shrugging her shoulders, pink wisp of brassiere falling from her trembling breasts. And with that unashamedly erotic picture branding my brain I suddenly noticed something else that shook my eyes.

She had removed her jacket in the bedroom, revealing the gray blouse which had been beneath it, and now I could see the voluptuously-rising mounds of her breasts under the blouse, their points thrusting against the thin cloth. I could see the curve, the hollow, the darker round shadow touching the cloth. And it was with an almost galvanizing shock I realized Eve was not wearing a brassiere.

The blouse was not transparent, but opaque, the material thin and silken, and beneath it the big firm silken breasts were bare. I shook my head, closed my eyes and thought: Wow, opened them and thought: *Wow*. Maybe Eve in the bedroom, instead of getting into something more comfortable, had gotten out of something less comfortable. And comfort was something I was practically out of.

"Boy!" I said. "Well, yes, sir, ma'am. That was a night, wasn't it?"

Something else had been on the tip of my tongue but when Eve leaned forward and — not aware of what she was doing, I presume — sort of wiggled her shoulders joyously from side to wild side, there was almost as much commotion under that blouse as two people kicking each other under a blanket.

Eve looked at me, green eyes almost glowing, lips parted in a smile, white teeth pressed together as if she were killing something between them, and enjoying it, and she said, "It *was* a fun night, Shell. Especially, once — once I let go."

She stretched her arms high over her head, then clenched her hands into fists and put them against the nape of her neck, arching her back, squirming slightly on the couch, moving her shoulders easily from side to side.

O.K., I couldn't help listening. And I was looking. True, I had only a few minutes before left Laurie, lovely Laurie Lee. But let's not be idiots; even a giddily ecstatic youth on his wedding afternoon will, should he surprisingly find himself in the midst of a nudist camp, glance around. At least glance one quick glance, one fleeting and surreptitious peek. That, heaven help them — us — is the nature of the beast. But, after all, I was only looking. So far, anyway.

Eve said, "Shell."

"Yes?"

"Why don't we . . ."

"Yeah?"

"Finish the . . . game ourselves. We wouldn't even have to start all over. We could take up where we left off."

"What . . . do you mean?"

She chuckled. "You know what I mean. We wouldn't even need cards — after all, I'd already lost everything. There wasn't anything more for me to lose."

Maybe that's what she thought.

She went on, "So it could be just . . . oh, a kind of Garden-of-Eden party." She smiled.

I smiled.

"You could be the first man . . . "

The hell I'd be the first man.

". . . and, after all, I'm Eve."

"But . . . but the snake is — "

"You could be — the devil!"

"I'd play hell!"

She laughed. "Let's do it. Let's play hell!"

"No."

"No?"

"Yes."

"You mean . . . yes?"

"No. I mean no."

Her eyes got colder. Everything seemed to get colder. She said, "You don't like the idea, then."

"Oh, it's a fine idea. It's just that, well, I have to go. I've got to run along. Really."

She was quiet for at least half a minute, chewing the inside of her lip, eyes slitted. Then she took a deep breath and said, "All right. It won't happen again. You can bet on that." She paused. "All right. Run along."

She sat there, steaming, chewing on her teeth and getting steamier by the second. Her half-full highball glass was on an end table near her and suddenly she picked it up and threw the drink in my face.

Well, I didn't sock her. It would take great, grave, and extreme provocation before I would sock a tomato. But the thought flitted through my skull like a rabid bat, I'll admit. I took a handkerchief from my pocket and, with what dignity I could muster, mopped my face. Then I got to my feet and stalked to the door.

"Shell. Wait, please."

Eve got up and came toward me, stopped in front of me. "I'm sorry. It was an impulse. I was — well, I'm sorry."

I shrugged. With dignity, I hoped.

"Really, Shell. I don't know what came over me. Don't stalk out like that."

"I wasn't stalking."

"You know what I mean. Friends, Shell? Forgiven? Please?"

I shrugged again. "Why not?"

I realized, then, that I really didn't give a hoot. Eve had a lovely face, and a body like those pictures that come in plain wrappers, but I looked upon her almost as if she were a shapely statue. Even when the four of us had been playing strip poker, I realized much of the stimulus and excitement for me had been because Laurie was there.

It was possible, of course, that kissing Laurie had used up all my juice, unzipped my zip, and so forth. Or that drink in my face dampened more than my chops. But whatever the reason, Eve struck me as a gal with all the electricity of a used flashlight battery. It just wasn't there. Whatever it is inside, whatever it is that flows. Eve sure had it on the outside, the shape of it, the form, the semblance, the design. But not the real thing. At least not for me.

So Eve and I smiled sappily at each other, and I turned and went out the door, and all the way down to the street, and all the way to my car, thinking about Laurie Lee.

Fifteen

I dropped off the papers at Jim's and jawed with him a bit, then drove back up Sunset to Vine and down Vine until it became North Rossmore.

The Spartan Apartment Hotel faces Rossmore, and sometimes I park in front. But the garages and open-air car slots are at the hotel's rear, so I drove back there.

I pulled into my slot, stepped out of the Cad onto the cement parking strip — and froze. Froze just for a moment, a split second. I'd either seen something or heard an unexpected sound, but I didn't wait to figure out what It was. I dived forward, dropping, jerking my right arm across my chest, slapping the butt of my gun.

Before I hit the cement, the night grew bright and sound blasted my ears. The light flared, lanced toward me from only ten yards away, from a spot across the narrow alley behind the hotel. The blast of the gun was hellishly loud, deep and booming. The flame was fat. Something ripped through muscle over my collarbone and I thought: Shotgun.

I pulled the Colt's trigger, pulled it again, aiming at the spot where that gush of flame had been. I fired twice more and then held my finger from the trigger, not yet knowing why. Then the thought came. There might be more than one man out there. If so, I didn't want to be sprawled here with an empty gun.

I heard a thump. That was all. No groans, no sound of movement. Somebody behind me in the hotel yelled. Lights came on, illuminating the whole area — and a man face down in the alley. He didn't move. As soon as the lights came on a car's engine, obviously already idling, roared. Immediately there was the screech of tires.

I jumped into the alley, looked to my left. Barely in time to see a flash of red as a car slid around to the left toward Rossmore. I didn't even see the car, just the taillight's flare.

"Shell?" It was somebody in the hotel's back doorway behind me.

I shouted over my shoulder, "Call the police! Shooting, car headed up Rossmore." A door slammed. I stepped to the prone man, rolled him over onto his back. The shotgun had been caught beneath him and I shoved it aside.

He was nobody I'd ever seen before. Two red stains discolored the khaki-brown shirt he wore. One of my slugs had hit him in the mouth, tearing through his lips and teeth and out the back of his neck. The way his head rolled loosely, the bullet must have crushed through vertebrae at the base of his skull, cut his spine.

That was why there'd been no sounds after he fell, no groans. He'd been dead in the air, his head flopping.

I could feel the slamming pulse in my throat, temples and wrists, feel it even in the backs of my legs. I licked my lips, surprised to find my mouth dry. I glanced around, stared down at the dead man.

Then there were cops, and more cops. Questions and more questions. Nobody, including me, had any idea who the gunman was. The police would check. Blood was running down my chest, soaking my shirt. One of the slugs from the shotgun had drilled through flesh and muscle near the base of my neck, on the left side just over the collarbone. It wasn't bad; at least it hadn't hit bone. Somebody put a bandage on it.

I was still standing in the alley with a police sergeant when a car pulled up near us and out of it stepped Lieutenant Wesley Simpson. The body hadn't been hauled to the morgue yet, and Wes walked over and looked down at the dead man, then stared at me, looked at the corpse some more.

Then he turned and, walking slowly, approached me.

"Hi, Wes," I said. "Old . . . friend."

"I got to sleep this time," he said, and his voice was that of a man with size six shoes on size ten feet, "was sleeping like a babe. How about that?"

"Wes, I didn't — "

"Dreaming, I was. Dreaming of sleeping. Then what do you think, Scott? The phone rang. Some guy had been shot — by Shell Scott. That's what the man told me." He paused. "You know what I said?"

"What did you say?"

"I said, 'No, you're kidding.'"

"I'm sorry, Wes. I guess I could have let the guy kill me. But you'd have had to come down anyway, wouldn't you?"

"Yeah." He nodded. "True. But that way it would have been more fun. Well, tell me the story."

I told him.

Then Wes said, "O.K. Come on along, we'll get it down on paper." And off I went to the slammer.

At seven o'clock in the morning I said to Wesley Simpson, "You know, the sunlight is starting to hurt my eyes."

He smiled. "It does that after a while, doesn't it?"

We were sitting in his office, drinking coffee. I had dictated and signed my statement and was now free to go. "Well, I guess I'll go home," I said.

"I'm not going home." Wes looked at his watch. "In just a little bit, I'll be on duty." He smiled horribly. "On duty. This that I'm doing now, last night, the night before, that's just my — my hobby."

"Yeah, it helps when you enjoy your work," I said. I stood up and stretched, grunting when I forgot the bandaged flesh wound. "Man, I feel like I could sleep a couple of days." I sighed. "But there'll be no sack time for me now. Not this late in the morning."

Wes peered at me from half-closed, slightly swollen, ghastly red eyes, and grinned. He didn't say a word, just grinned. When I went out, he was still grinning.

Back in my apartment I fixed some breakfast, which was mostly coffee plus a few spoonfuls of lousy mush. You'd think after all this time I could cook edible oatmeal, but almost invariably it comes out a thin gruel or a lump of gunk you could drive a nail with. Not that it makes much difference. With my morning appetite, I don't even like the slop when it's good.

During the morning the police identified the man I'd killed last night, through a teletype kickback from the F.B.I. He was an out-of-state hood with a long record, including arrests for ADW, manslaughter, and first-degree murder. He'd served one prison term in Illinois for a murder a dozen years ago. He was not a California hood, and had never been known to be in California prior to this time.

I talked to Feeney in Narcotics and asked if there was anything new on the alleged shipment of Da Da Baby Food from Brea Island to San

Pedro. Police had determined there was a shipment due this afternoon, from Handi-Foods, destined for the M.W. Wilson warehouse. It wouldn't arrive at the dock until about four P.M., however, and I told Feeney I'd call him again after that time.

About ten A.M. Wesley Simpson called me. "Just got this from Central, Shell. I think they've got the body of this Michael Grauschtunger downtown. Somebody scraped out a shallow grave, rolled him in it and covered him up. Must've been in a hurry, because part of one foot stuck out a little and a couple kids playing Gunsmoke spotted it. Told their parents and they called in. Anyway, some dead guy's in the morgue."

"You're not sure it's Mickey?"

"Well, pretty sure. We figure it is because we got records on him showing he'd had an appendectomy, knife scar on his side, and a mole in the middle of his back, and these all match the corpse. But — try this, Shell — the dead guy's face was bashed in something awful, besides which somebody used a knife to slash most of the flesh off his fingers, especially the tips."

"Whoever dumped him would take out insurance against hangnails. Even if Mickey happened to be found they didn't want anybody identifying the mugg, and maybe tracing him back to whoever put him up to the job."

He told me I got a cigar, and I said, "But, hell, Wes, I put some slugs into the little man. You've got the .32 down there. Dig the pills out and compare — "

"That's the cutey, Shell. They've *been* dug. He's cut up pretty good, and the bullets are no longer in Mickey M."

I didn't speak for a few seconds. Finally, I said, "Cutey is the word. This guy is so cute he'd wear a belt and suspenders and still hang onto his pants."

"Well, get down to the morgue and identify him. If you can. But maybe you better not eat first."

Fortunately, I have a strong stomach. Corpses are never pleasant, but the way this one had been hacked up, even I was glad I hadn't forced down a whole bowl of mush this morning. It was difficult for me to make positive identification, but I declared that the deceased was Michael M. Grauschtunger, then left the morgue.

My last stop before lunch was to see Ralph Merle. We talked for several minutes and I paid him an exorbitant fee, but the vital item of info was that Drake Patterson had, indeed, entered that $80,000 on his 1955 tax return.

After a rare steak and some vegetables which very definitely tasted unorganic, I went back to the Spartan, arriving in my apartment a little after noon. Earlier I had phoned Jim and told him about the episode in the alley; now I gave him another call and filled him in on the new items I'd gathered.

He whistled. "The little guy had really been carved up, huh?"

"He had. It looked as if an amateur surgeon, and a roaring sadist to boot, had worked on him. Anyway, we already knew who the guy was."

"It gets queerer and queerer."

"Yeah. Want me to pick you up, Jim?"

"No, I'll meet you at Beiglen's. About twelve-thirty."

"Right."

"See you there, then." I heard something in the background, partly drowned out by the sound of his voice. Then I said so long, and the receiver clicked. I stood there a moment trying to figure out what the sound had been. Then I got it. Probably it had been that bing-bong-*clong* of his door chimes. Somebody calling? If so, it must have been somebody Jim expected; anyway, he hadn't mentioned it.

I got a jar of finely-cut fresh shrimp out of the refrigerator and sprinkled some on top of the water in both aquariums. One is a small aquarium filled with frisky guppies, and the other a twenty-gallon community tank. The fish gobbled the flakes of shrimp, darting through clumps of feathery Myriophyllum and waving strands of light-green Cabomba. Very pretty.

I said, "Hello, fish." Sometimes I talk to them like that. O.K., so I like fish. But it also remains true that there is a strangely peaceful world in a twenty-gallon tank of water populated by little striped Zebras and translucent Glassfish and radiantly glowing Neons. I watch them, I enjoy them, I forget — and I relax. It's as simple as that.

I would have liked to watch them longer, but today was not the day. I said so long to the fish, and went out once more, into the world populated by people.

It was quite a wrench.

Sixteen

Someone was already playing the organ. The dolorous, quavering tones floated from the open doors of Beiglen's Mortuary, squirmed through sunlight and over the grass, oozed against my ears as I parked my Cad at the curb.

It was twelve-thirty, half an hour before the services were to begin.

The organ music bugged me. I also loathe organ music and the sad, sorrowful songs organs seem always to play. Give me the gay songs — even at funerals. But the organ music went on, writhing in the air like worms.

I went up the steps and inside. It was cool. The air smelled dusty. I looked around but didn't see Jim, so I stepped to the door of the chapel, where services would be held. Several people were seated; the casket rested in stiff rigidity at the front of the room, masses of flowers banked around it; but Jim wasn't in sight.

A thought crawled into my mind, wriggling like the tones of the organ. I remembered hearing, in the moment before Jim had hung up the phone, that merry bing-bong-*clong* of his living-room chimes. Somebody at the door then. Probably a delivery of some kind, could be a lot of things. There wasn't anything to worry about. But that cold thought moved, grew a little.

I found a phone in the hallway near the front doors, dialed. Jim's phone rang, rang again, unanswered. People were coming through the doors, walking slowly, silently. The services would start soon. Maybe Jim was on his way, driving here right now. Maybe. But I wasn't going to wait any longer. I went outside, sprinted to my car. I drove too fast up Sunset, barely made two lights before they turned red. At Jim's I jumped out, leaving the Cad's door open, and went up the wooden steps three at a time, jumped up the curving ramp.

The front door wasn't quite closed. There was about a quarter of an inch between door and frame. Now that I was here, for some reason I moved slowly, raising my hand and pressing it against the door.

The door swung inward a few inches and stopped.

Right then I knew.

I hadn't seen him yet. But I knew.

I pushed the door gently, easing it open enough so I could slip through. Then I shut it behind me. Jim lay on his back, the long rangy length of him slanting down the three steps, head lower than his body, feet near the door. His eyes were closed. There was a red stain on his white shirt, and a thin wet line of red ran from the corner of his mouth up past one eye and into his black hair.

I knelt by him, put a hand on the side of his face. "Jim," I said. "Jim."

His skin was warm. I felt something move beneath my palm. Then his lips twitched, his eyelids fluttered.

"*Jim!*" I said, my voice loud in the empty room.

His eyes opened, and he looked at me. The lids blinked once, then he looked at me again, kept his eyes open. "Hang on, pal," I said. "We'll make it." I got up, jumped to the phone and dialed the operator.

"Emergency," I said, trying to keep my voice down, trying to speak slowly. "Emergency. A man has been shot. Send an ambulance and the police." I gave the address, waited until the operator repeated it in calm tones, and hung up.

Kneeling by Jim again I said, "It'll be O.K., pal . . . Troops are on the way. It's going to be all right." The same old words. "It's going to be all right." But in my mind I was swearing, cursing everything including myself. I couldn't help saying, "Sorry I wasn't here, Jim."

His lips moved. His mouth opened.

"Just take it easy," I told him. "There'll be an ambulance here in a minute."

He kept trying to speak, forced sounds from his mouth. Sounds and another small trickle of blood. I could see, where the coat had fallen away from his shirt, the spot where the bullet had entered. It was dead center, but low.

Sounds from his mouth again. And I knew Jim would keep trying until he passed out, or died. Trying, undoubtedly, to tell me who had shot him. Because, unless this time again it was a hired gun like the man dead in the alley last night, that could be the answer to everything, could at least lead to the answer.

So I tried to make it easy for him.

"One word," I said, "Just one word, Jim, if you know it. Just tell me the man's name."

I leaned close. His eyes widened a little and he sucked air into his nostrils. His face seemed paler, but he was straining, making a terrible effort to speak. His voice was faint, thin and weak but clear enough.

"It . . . wasn't a man," he said.

Seventeen

Jim's eyelids fluttered, and with the last of his strength he said, "It — " he choked. "It . . . was Lor — " Then he stopped moving. His mouth went slack. But his lids closed over his eyes. They hadn't stayed open, staring.

I felt for his pulse. It was still there, thready, but there, the heart still beating. I heard sirens.

The shock was delayed, perception slow. My thoughts moved sluggishly at first.

I was thinking of what Jim had said. "It was Lor — " He had almost certainly, I thought, started to say, "It was Lorimer." It stunned me. The vision of that chubby pink face, the remembered sounds of his too-delicate words, rose in my mind. It seemed incredible, but killers come in all kinds of packages, some of them even more incredible than the thought of Horace Lorimer as a murderer.

And it was then, finally, that it hit me.

"It wasn't a man," he had said. But Lorimer was a man. So it couldn't have been Lorimer. But nothing else made sense. If it wasn't a man, then it had to be a woman, and that not only eliminated Lorimer, but Lou Grecian, hired hoodlums, half the population. The only women involved in this mess — so far as I knew, anyway — were Laurie and Eve, and the other four models from Alexandria's. But I'd hardly said a word to the other four, nor had Aaron or Jim — not in my presence, at least. Hell, it could be a woman I'd never seen, never even heard of.

I was still trying to figure it out when the ambulance — and once again the police — arrived.

I rolled the Cad's windows down and drove, letting the wind rush over my face, hoping it would pull me wider awake, clear my brain.

110

My eyes were heavy, my whole shoulder and the side of my neck were sore, and I felt rocky and feverish, hungry for sleep.

The ambulance attendants had been giving Jim plasma when they drove away. By now he would be in the hospital, in the operating room. He might live; he might not. It would be hours before I would know.

I hadn't told the police what Jim had said. Because I didn't really know, or wouldn't believe I knew. I was sure Jim must have started to say "Lorimer." It seemed to me, now, that he had said "Lori" or "Lorim" because with the last of his breath his lips had closed. As if he'd said "Lorim . . . " Then his jaw had sagged and he'd fallen into unconsciousness.

The more I thought about it the less clear it became. It was as if I had a mental block in that one area, thoughts veering away from it, as if I didn't want to think about it. I shoved it all from my mind and drove without conscious direction. I was on Wilshire Boulevard, headed toward L.A. by this time, on the Miracle Mile. I passed swank men's clothing stores on my right, dress shops and automobile agencies on the opposite side of the wide boulevard, tall office buildings. Then, the big department stores. The May Company and Ohrbach's, with the La Brea Tar Pits, between them. The name made me think of Brea Island, and I wondered about that can of mashed bananas, wondered if it was really heroin, or only — mashed bananas.

A block farther was the Standish, where Horace Lorimer lived, where we'd had our talk, where he'd told me of defrauding the U.S. Government of taxes due it under the law. Legally Lorimer was a kind of monster; morally, not really such a monster as all that. If, that is, he was honest in other ways. Of course, maybe he was a monster in all kinds of ways. Could be, I thought, could be.

I was going along like that, just muddling apparently inconsequential nothings in my noodle, when the idea ripped through me like a 220-volt current. I slammed my foot on the brake pedal in an involuntary reflex, my back pressing into the seat behind me.

The Cad skidded. Behind me a horn blared, I heard the squeal of another car's tires blending with the sound of my own sliding on the street. Whoever was behind me couldn't stop quite in time and gently nudged my rear bumper. A man yelled, swearing, calling me names — deserved names undoubtedly.

I pulled over to the curb, found a parking spot. A white-faced guy in a Buick drove slowly past, leaning toward his right-hand window and bellowing at me. I didn't mind. I barely noticed. Little explosions were going off in my head.

Forgotten for the moment were Jim and the funeral. Instead, other things marched through my mind. I knew Lorimer's tax fraud had been workable, slick and carefully planned; Aaron had received $50,000 merely for signing his name — but he'd signed once, refused to sign a second time when Lorimer asked him, urged him to. He'd refused to "resell" the island to Lorimer, or Lorimer's company — the company in which Grecian was involved, Grecian and Mickey M. and men like them, who would kill a guy for sneezing. Aaron wouldn't have refused to resell merely to keep the fifty G's, because he would have kept the fifty G's anyway; that was his payoff.

No, Aaron Paradise must have wanted the island itself, Brea Island, so badly he was willing to risk a great deal, even his life, in order to keep it. And drifting into my thoughts now were a dozen other things I'd seen and heard but hadn't put together, and into the middle of it all had come the one word which shook the pieces into place.

That word was: Brea.

Brea Island, sure. But it is also a most familiar name to a lot of people, especially to nearly everybody in the L.A.-Hollywood area. Because right on busy Wilshire Boulevard is the very well known spot called the La Brea Tar Pits, which I had just driven past. There's even a city near Los Angeles named Brea.

It's a Spanish word. I remembered Ralph Merle casually mentioning that Brea Island had once been owned by the Spanish. *Brea* Island, the city of *Brea*. And *La Brea* Tar Pits — a redundant name when spoken in both Spanish and English, because in the Spanish *brea* means "tar."

And tar often means: Oil.

It had meant that in Los Angeles. And how it had meant that. The La Brea Pits were, in the 1890's, the scene of one of the wildest booms in the history of oil exploration. Within a few years thousands of wells were drilled right here on part of what is now the fabulous "Miracle Mile" — into an enormous pool of oil. And it had been found because one man, named Doheny, a mining prospector, saw a wagon loaded with tar rumbling along a Los Angeles street and asked the driver where it came from. The driver told him: the Brea Pits.

So Doheny and his partner went to the Pits and dug a hole in the ground. At 165 feet, oil started to flow. Only seven barrels a day then, but that was merely the first trickle from a pool that would eventually produce more than seventy million barrels of oil.

Aaron Paradise had been a wildcatter, was an experienced oilman, and he would sure as hell have known the Doheny story, known what the word Brea meant — or might mean. Just the name, of course, didn't mean much. Not by itself. But there was all Jim had told me about his brother, his studies in geology and petroleum engineering, the wells he'd drilled; there was the sight of Jim crawling from beneath that bunkhouse — in which were the filthy, grease-stained, oil-blackened sheets and blankets — with oil on his hands and trousers; the peculiar conglomeration of pipes and valves in the sealed-off part of the bunkhouse, not connected to anything, capped in some way; there was that large area around the bunkhouse which had been bulldozed, leveled — or covered over with earth.

I thought of other things, and suddenly wanted very much to have another talk with Horace Lorimer.

But first there was somebody else I wanted to talk to. I didn't know his name yet, but it took me only ten minutes to find him. The second office-building lobby I checked listed on its register the name, "Farwell and Klein — Farlein Drilling and Exploration Co., Inc."

I found the office, went in, and in another minute was talking to Ed Klein. He was a wide-shouldered man of about sixty, a fuzz of gray hair covering his scalp, with brown eyes and the steady, quiet gaze that you sometimes see in sailors who spend long months on the sea. His face had been lined by weather and baked deep brown by the sun, and he wore a white shirt open at the neck, rolled up over bulging forearms corded with still-hard muscle.

I didn't beat around the bush. I told him what I'd seen and guessed, and finished it up with, "Does it sound like there might be oil on Brea Island?"

He opened his desk drawer, took out a cigar, bit off the end and spat it into a wastebasket, then slowly pushed the drawer shut. "Well, I'm an old wildcatter myself, Mr. Scott. The only thing you can say for sure about finding oil is: Oil's where you find it." He struck a match, puffed on the cigar. "But it sure sounds like you got a well out there." He blew some smoke in the air. "Describe those pipes and all again."

I told him once more, as accurately as my memory permitted.

"That there is a Christmas tree, Mr. Scott," he said. "Sure, it must be a well, all right."

"What's a Christmas tree? — and keep it simple."

He smiled. "That's just a name for what you call the pipes and valves at the top of the well's casing. It's so you can control the flow of oil, cut it down or shut it off." He drew a picture in the air before him with his cigar. "At the bottom you've got the biggest pipe, maybe a foot and a half diameter, and a valve or two, then she goes up" — he lifted his cigar — "to a There, say, with a couple of more valves, more pipe. Higher up she goes, the smaller the pipes and valves get. Looks kind of like a metal Christmas tree, which is where the name comes from."

That was it. That was what Jim and I had seen.

Klein said, "What in hell did he have it all boarded up for, like you said. Was he trying to hide the damn thing?"

I nodded, "Yeah, that's what he was doing. Only he didn't hide it well enough."

"A Christmas tree's a pretty big thing to hide, Mr. Scott."

"Uh-huh. This thing went up six or eight feet above ground. I guess he did the best he could." While puzzling over Aaron's attempt to hide the evidence, I said, "Mr. Klein, when a well comes in, is that what you call a gusher? Oil all over the place, all over the ground?"

"Well, that was mostly in the old days. That was because of the gas pressure pushing the oil up, sending it up in the air, clear over the rig — yeah, all over the place. But it's not likely you'll see a gusher in California any more." He sounded a little sad. "Most of that pressure's gone, all been let loose now. You got to pump now, pump the oil up." He shifted his cigar, chewed on it. "On this island way out there, though, it could be. Could be plenty of pressure down there."

He leaned back in his chair and looked up toward the ceiling. "Nothing like a gusher. Nothing in the world like that feeling. I've brought a few in, and the funny thing, Mr. Scott, is that when she blows you get the best damn feeling, and it's not the money you're thinking about. It's a kind of — victory. It's like you dug down there with your bare hands, like it was there waiting for you, and fighting you every inch, and you licked it."

He suddenly sat up straighter. "Maybe that don't make a bit of sense to you."

"It makes a hell of a lot of sense." I grinned at him and he grinned back. In a way, he made me think of Drake Patterson. I hoped it wasn't a vanishing race; it was the only race I wanted to belong to.

Klein said, "I'd sure like to see one more. I'd even like to see this rig out there on the island."

I looked at my watch. It was only twenty minutes after two in the afternoon; it wouldn't be dark for another six hours or so. I said, "Matter of fact, I'd very much appreciate it if you'd go to Brea with me, look the place over, tell me what really is out there. I might be able to make it later this afternoon, and if you'll go along with me you can name your fee."

He chewed on the cigar. "Well, since it sounds kind of interesting, you pay me fifty dollars and I'll be glad to check it over for you."

Five minutes later I got up to leave. I'd mentioned Jim's boat, but that was too slow for Ed Klein, and he said he had half a dozen friends who owned planes, including one who owned a seaplane. He'd told me to phone him when and if I was ready to go and he'd meet me off Balboa, adjacent to Newport Beach. *Off* Balboa — I was to have somebody take me off shore in a boat and the plane would set down and pick me up.

It sounded a little tricky to me, but I was reassured by Klein's casual acceptance of it all. Apparently the plane's owner was a marvelous pilot. I was halfway out the door before the thought hit me. I stopped and said, "Oh, oh."

"What's the matter?"

I had just remembered those baby-food manufacturers.

I explained to Klein the kind of men who were on the island, not trying to make them sound any less horrible than they actually were, and finished, "So we'd better make it another day."

He grinned. "Somehow you don't strike me as a man who'd let a little thing like that stop you from — "

"A *little* thing? There must be a dozen of those apes out there, at least. Probably more."

He grinned. "Son, I was in Hogtown in '17 and '18 — when they changed the name to Desdemona — clear through to the end, and there was never a boom like that before or since. I'll bet you a pint of

Old Crow I've seen more dead men than you have. I was eighteen years old when the Hogtown well blew out and caught fire, and I was nineteen when I got shot for the first time. Spilled a roughneck's drink by accident and he shot me on purpose. Knocked me clean off my feet. But I got up and killed him." He knocked ash off his cigar. "You want to go out there, I'll go with you."

I just looked at him for a few seconds, then grinned. "Ed, I'd be afraid not to go now. If nothing goes wrong in the next hour or two, I'll give you that call."

He nodded, leaned back and put his feet on the desk, and I went out.

Horace Lorimer wasn't in the Standish Hotel and it took me twenty minutes and a ten-dollar bill to find out where he might be. The ten spot went to the doorman in front of the Standish, who told me he'd brought Lorimer's black Lincoln Continental over from the lot an hour or more ago and Lorimer had driven off in it. He added that Horace often visited a joint called the Purple Room, and gave me the address. For free, he gave me Lorimer's license number.

The Purple Room was on a side street a couple of blocks off Wilshire, a cocktail lounge I'd never been in, hadn't even seen before. But across the street, in the club's parking lot, was Lorimer's black Continental. I drove a block past the club, pulled around the corner and parked. For a few seconds I let my head rest against the back of the car's seat and closed my eyes. It was almost like getting sapped. My lids tried to stick together, and the blackness was warm and comfortable, a welcome blackness I could have dived into for a good twelve hours, or more. But I pried my eyes open, stretched my face around and yawned, then walked back to the club, under the awning, and into the Purple Room.

Places, like people, seem to have their own aura, a vibration, their own "feel," something almost tangible which affects the senses. Whether that's true or not, this Purple Room sure gave me a queer message.

I stopped inside the door, and I hadn't stood there more than ten seconds before my spine started to bristle. I couldn't see much. The place was not quite as dark as a tomb. I could hear voices, soft, subdued, murmuring. Then I heard the light tinkle of a piano. I felt — well, a little creepy, ill at ease, uncomfortable. And I didn't know why. The air was a bit sweet and stuffy, that was all.

My eyes became adjusted to the gloom and I could see people sitting at tables, drinking and talking. I stepped forward, perched on the edge of a chair beside a small empty table and looked around. The piano was at the end of the room on my right, about twenty feet away; small tables filled the space between and lined the walls. Directly ahead stretched a bar, from behind which two bartenders in purple jackets served the half-dozen customers occupying stools. Hell, it was just an ordinary cocktail lounge, doing a good early afternoon business. I even recognized one of the bartenders, a guy named Jerry something or other.

I hadn't known Jerry here, though. I'd met him at another bar — in San Francisco, I remembered, a year or two back when I'd been working on a case, the nature of which escaped me at the moment. We'd had a couple of long conversations, a few drinks together.

I got up, started toward the bar, and stopped. I'd just had the jarring impression that I'd seen Eve Angers. I looked again. On my right, about halfway between the piano bar and where I stood, at a table against the wall near me, sat a black-haired gal talking to another woman. The one with her back to me looked like Eve. The other woman was — well, she was weird. Her hair was as blonde as Eve's was black, almost white-blonde hair that fell inches beneath her shoulders, but it hung completely straight, without a hint of wave or curl, as limp and lifeless as a wig made of thin spaghetti. She was thin herself, angular, her mouth a straight slash without makeup. It was a face like skin stretched over bone, a face to be presented only to steel mirrors, like the face on the bride of Death. I shuddered, really shuddered, looking at her.

I moved across the room to the bar, a bit nervously, because for some reason I didn't want to be seen, not by anybody who knew me. I didn't know why for sure; I just knew I didn't want to be seen. Tension built up in me gradually, rose along my spine and gathered in a knot at the base of my skull. I could see the black-haired gal now. It was Eve, all right. Across from her the other woman, with hair like thin strips from a shroud, smiled at Eve, talked to her, smiled.

My head throbbed; I could feel heat at the spot where the shotgun pellet had hit me last night; I wondered if I could be in some kind of shock, induced by the wound, the lack of sleep and rest, the emotional hammering of these last few days, and even hours.

I looked around. At men and women, sitting at tables, drinking, talking. There seemed nothing unusual. But then the scene seemed to shift. It was the same — yet different. I had looked right at it, it was there in front of my eyes, but it hadn't impressed me until now. Men and women were sitting at tables, true; but at no table was a man sitting with a woman.

There were two women at a table, three, even women alone. And men alone and together. But not one man with a woman. I glanced up. At the end of the piano bar sat Horace Lorimer, a pink cocktail in front of him, leaning toward the male piano player. The piano player sang, showing a lot of flashing white teeth, singing, "Thank Heaven for little — boys . . ." and smiling at Horace, smiling at Horace Lorimer.

Glasses tinkled behind me and I turned to the bar. Jerry was rinsing some glasses, swishing them through tubs of water. I caught his eye, motioned with my head. He frowned, then recognition showed on his face.

On my left, at the end of the room opposite the piano bar, a purple-draped doorway led into another room. I pointed toward it and Jerry nodded. I walked into the other room and waited. The room was empty, chairs stacked on top of the tables. In one wall were two doors, marked "Girls" and "Boys." I supposed they were rest-rooms.

In two or three minutes Jerry joined me. We stood inside the purple draperies at the door and he said, "Shell Scott, isn't it?" I nodded and he said, "Gee, it's been a couple years, hasn't it?"

"That's right. You still enjoy picking up a buck, Jerry?"

He grinned. "You know it."

"A double sawbuck, say?"

"For what?"

I pulled back the drape with one hand and pointed. "The guy at the end of the piano bar. You know him?"

"Old fatstuff? Sure . . . Lorimer. What about him?"

"You've seen him in here before, then?"

"Sure, a lot of times, regular hangout. But I knew him and his wife in San Francisco before, served them there lots of times when I was at Lupo's. You remember Lupo's."

The name jogged my memory; that was the bar where I'd met Jerry.

He was going on, "He's been here a lot, but it's only this last week or so he's come in with his wife."

"With his wife? They've both come here?"

"Sure, he and Gerda only been in together a couple of times. Never sit together, though. Just like now." He yawned, bored with eccentricity.

"She's here?" Lorimer had told me, I remembered that his wife's name was Gerda; but he'd also said she was in San Francisco.

Jerry stifled his yawn, nodded, and pointed. He was pointing straight at the table where Eve sat, straight at the curse of death, at one of hell's harlots, at the white-blonde weirdo. "That's Gerda," he said.

She looked like a Gerda, I thought, and I said, with massive understatement, "Not much to look at, is she?"

"Who looks?" he said. "Who looks at the pigs?"

And that snatched up another bit of memory — the case I'd been on when I met Jerry. It had been a crime of passion: one young boy, who waited on tables at Lupo's, had killed another young boy, crushing in his skull with a gold-plated miniature of the Hermes of Praxiteles. It had struck me as strange that Jerry would have known Lorimer at Lupo's and be here, now, in the Purple Room. But it wasn't so strange after all. There wouldn't be many bars like this; and Lupo's was a bar like this.

Confusion tangled my thoughts. What the hell? Why would Eve be here, talking to Gerda — to Horace Lorimer's wife? Why was she here at all?

Lorimer sipped at his pink drink then slid off his stool, started to walk this way. Probably coming back here to the Boys' room.

"Jerry, is there a back way out of here?"

"Sure, parking lot in back. Some of the customers don't like to come in the front way."

"Show me." Lorimer had stopped at the table, was speaking to Gerda. Then he said something to Eve and headed this way again. I got a twenty-dollar bill from my wallet, handed it to Jerry as he started toward the back of the room.

He opened a door and I went through it, saying, "You didn't see me, Jerry. I wasn't here."

He nodded and closed the door behind me. Just before it shut I saw Lorimer step past the purple drapery. I looked around, at ten or a dozen cars, Eve's white T-Bird among them. At the back of the lot was an alley. I walked to it, then trotted to my Cad.

Twenty minutes later Lorimer came out under the awning in front of the Purple Room. He was alone. I was parked half a block away, pointed toward Wilshire Boulevard. The attendant got Lorimer's car for him; he got in and drove toward Wilshire. I followed him. He left his car at the curb in front of the Standish, went into the hotel. By the time I'd parked and followed him in he was out of sight. But the elevator needle rose to point at the top floor, the penthouse suites.

When the elevator reached the lobby again I climbed in. It was self-service, and I pushed the top button, the cage moved upward. Thoughts turned and tumbled in my head. The elevator stopped, the doors opened. I stepped out into a short hallway fronting the two penthouse suites. Lorimer's was on the right. I stepped to his door, pushed the button.

One soft sound, like a gong, boomed inside the suite.

The knob clicked, the door opened.

And she stood there, wearing a linen sheath in light chartreuse, a shade that almost matched her eyes.

And her hair wasn't white — it was black.

Eve.

Eighteen

I didn't really react.

There had been, I guess, too many shocks to my nervous system in the last few hours. Or maybe this, and all it meant, had to fuse somewhere inside me, sink in, pull the rest of the pattern together.

Whatever the reason, I simply stood there, feeling numb, staring at Eve. She seemed shocked, but recovered and spoke first.

"Shell, what in the world are you doing here? What do you want?" But she spoke — or it seemed to me she spoke — very slowly, an appreciable pause between the words, each word individually spaced and surrounded by its measure of silence.

I didn't say anything, stepped forward pushing the door wider. She moved back, then turned and walked over the lavender carpet toward the white divan where Lorimer and I had sat last night. Her coat lay across the back of the divan, the big black bag on the floor near it.

She was saying, speaking more briskly now, "This is the strangest thing — your coming here, I mean. I just came up to see Horace, I've only been here once before, but I had to ask him something. And then *you* show up." She stopped by the divan, bent and picked up the black bag, turned to face me.

I walked up to her, stopped a couple of feet away. Eve was fumbling with the leather drawstrings at the top of the bag, pulling it open. She reached into the bag for something, but Horace Lorimer was just stepping through an open doorway, wearing a magnificently beaded and embroidered robe, white silk or satin glowing with color, vibrant with beads and threads of red and blue and gold and green. He might have been a prince of Xanadu or Samarkand, except for the round, fat, pink Kris-Kringle face.

He saw me the instant I turned. He stopped, his mouth dropped open, and he screamed. It was faint but piercing, high and piercing, the way a startled woman might scream. Without a moment's hesitation he spun around and jumped back into the room.

Then, it happened. In that split second. Something happened to time — in much the same way time had been distorted, speeded up, in the strange film Jim had made. Something seemed to dissolve in my brain, not merely in imagination but as though an actual physical change, or melting, occurred in one small group of cells. Everything that had happened, all I'd heard and done and seen in these last days, was present now, immediate, before me; dozens of scattered pieces fused into a thing without crack or crevice, every part fitting where it belonged, and I knew it all.

I turned fast, swinging my left arm up, balling my fist. I didn't try to pull the punch, I was trying to knock her head off. My fist landed on her temple, a glancing blow, not solid, but solid enough. She was unconscious as she fell.

And I was just in time. Barely in time. She didn't quite, not quite, have time to pull the trigger.

The gun she'd taken from her black bag fell, bounced on the carpet. I picked it up. Lorimer was still making noises as he scurried back into the living room, high, frantic, hysterical noises. He burst from the door into the living room. A frightened, wild, hysterical fat man. He had a small gun in his right hand.

He might have been able to hit me with a bullet from that little gun. I don't know. I didn't think much about it. I shot him four times, once in the chest and three times in the head.

I waited until Eve stirred, moaned, and slowly sat up.

Then I said quietly, "It's over. I just killed your husband, Gerda."

Nineteen

Eve's green eyes strayed from me to the body of Horace Lorimer, prone on the lavender carpet. Then she looked at my face again and said, "Is he . . . dead?"

"You bet he's dead. As dead as Aaron Paradise."

"You *killed* him," she said, looking once more at Lorimer's body. "Why? Why, Shell — "

"Oh, knock it off, Eve. Or Gerda — keep it Eve between us old friends, O.K.?"

"You must be out of your — "

"I told you to knock it off," I said mildly. "I know what you did and why you did it, Eve. I know you killed Aaron Paradise. Yourself, I mean, with your hand wrapped around the gun, your finger on the trigger. I know why you came to our little party Saturday night. I know you shot Jim — in fact he told me you did. In a way. I know about the narcotics racket, the oil on Brea Island — the Christmas tree — hell, all of it, sweetheart. So just sit there and think about that for a minute. And when it sinks in, we'll have a little chat."

With every sentence I spoke, her face grew more drawn and pale, grew older. Even with the lines more prominent, though, and strain pulling at her face, she was beautiful — on the outside, anyway. Inside, she was a hell of a mess.

I hadn't paid much attention before to how Eve was dressed, but it was as if a body like those pictures you see in *Cavalier* were to be dressed in something from *Vogue*. Her form-fitting pale-chartreuse sheath had an extremely low square neckline, exposing rounded whiteness and soft deep cleft, but somehow the sight failed to drive me wild.

At the divan's left, next to the table on which sat the sculpture of the nude guy holding a baby and some grapes, two tan suitcases rested on the lavender carpet. They were open now, because I'd already gone through them, finding items of Eve's clothing, zippy underthings, two pairs of shoes. That was all — but she'd been packed for travel.

Eve looked at the open suitcases, at dead Horace, then at me. But she tried again. "I didn't . . . kill Aaron," she said. Her eyes shifted. "It was Horace."

"Eve, quit trying. When the police get here a quick check will prove you're Horace Lorimer's wife, from San Francisco, that there isn't anybody called Eve Angers." I took the revolver which had been in her handbag from my coat pocket and held it toward her. "This gun — which you tried to shoot me in the back with — is probably the gun you used on Jim this afternoon. If so, ballistics tests can prove it." I dropped the revolver into my pocket again and said, "More important, Jim Paradise is still alive."

She was quiet for a long time. Finally she sighed. "Jim isn't dead?"

I shook my head — hoping he wasn't.

That seemed to do it. Eve slumped; the flesh of her face appeared to sag. She sighed again. "How much time do I have before the police get here?"

"I haven't called them yet. But I'm going to right now."

Before Eve had come to I had picked up Lorimer's little chrome-plated .32 automatic and dropped it, also, into a coat pocket, then checked the suite to make sure nobody else was in it. After that I'd phoned the Loma Drive Receiving Hospital. Jim had still been in surgery, with a fifty-fifty chance to come out alive. A second call had been to the Narcotics Division. Captain Feeney and some of his men had left for San Pedro more than two hours earlier to check on that can of Da Da bananas; if narcotics were found, they would go straight to Brea Island — but there'd been no word from Feeney yet. I had just started to call Homicide and ask that a team be sent up here when Eve had moaned and stirred, so I'd hung up the phone and walked over to her.

Eve slowly straightened up, and for long seconds her eyes were cold and hard and bright. But then the dullness filled her green eyes again and her shoulders slumped. "I guess the party's really ended," she said.

"It's ended."

She slowly got to her feet, looked at me. "Well, let's get it over with," she said. She turned and walked quickly to the phone on a stand against the wall. I started after her. She dialed, but I wasn't close enough to see whether she'd dialed the "0" or the "9" next to it. If she'd dialed "9", of course, nobody would be on the other end of the line. I let her go ahead, wondering what she was trying to pull, if anything.

But I heard noises in the receiver, then she spoke, and merely said, "Operator, get me the police." After a pause she said, "Please send the police to the Standish Hotel on Wilshire." She listened, then said, "Just send some officers to Horace Lorimer's suite," and hung up, turned to face me and with an odd smile on her face said, flatly, "That's it. Like springing the trap while you stand on it, isn't it? Or dropping your own cyanide into the acid?" She took a deep breath. "Well, we — I — haven't much time. I'll make you a trade, Shell."

"What kind of trade?"

"Tell me how you guessed the truth, and I'll tell you what I did and how I did it. Anything you want."

She walked briskly back to the couch and sat down at its end, next to the statuette of the nude man, put out her left hand and idly caressed the gleaming bronze. I sat next to her and said, "Including Aaron?"

"Including Aaron."

"O.K.," I said. "But it was more than a guess. I wasn't really onto you, personally, until I saw you in the Purple Room a little while ago." Her eyes widened. "Yeah, I was there," I said. "While you were talking to Frankenstein's monster's mother, or whoever she was. A bartender pointed out Gerda, Lorimer's wife, and I thought he was pointing at the Bat-Woman, not at you. I didn't get it until everything hit me all at once, bang, just a little while ago. But I guess the key was realizing you hung around places like the Purple Room — and Lupo's. Well, if *that* was your meat, why ask for poison? Why would you agree to come to a party with Jim and me Saturday night? A party at which there was, perish the thought, the possibility of strip poker — if, of course, Jim happened to be still alive — strip poker with *men*."

Hate flickered in her cat-green eyes, bare and obvious. She could hate me openly now. Slowly and deliberately she said, "You rotten bastard." Without even an "oops" this time.

"That's the stuff," I said. "Be yourself for a change. Well, let's look at the murder of Aaron. He'd been in bed with a woman before he was killed. The police — and I — assumed the killer waited outside till she left, then came in and shot Aaron in bed. But after a while that didn't fit. For one thing, it was a contact wound. You know what a contact wound is, don't you, Eve?"

She didn't say anything.

"It means the gun was touching his flesh. A killer walking in from outside wouldn't have got that close to the man. And a professional wouldn't stop with one shot, by the way."

She stared at me, not speaking.

I went on. "The glasses were wiped clean. The unknown killer wouldn't have done that — but the woman who drank from one of those glasses and then shot Aaron would have. You would have, Eve. Sure, you had sense enough to wipe both glasses, not merely your own, but it was still a mistake."

"Anything else you can impress me with? — I'm not being sarcastic, Shell. I am impressed."

Flattery, I thought; who needs it? "That's enough for a start," I said.

"All right. What do you want to know? For a start."

"How did Lorimer find out about the oil on Brea Island? I know Aaron's reason for refusing to transfer title back to Horace was because he'd found oil on Brea, and I can even understand why Horace wanted *both* Aaron and Jim killed once Aaron refused to sell."

Surprisingly, her lips had curved into a smile. She really seemed amused, though I couldn't think of anything I'd said that was even mildly amusing. I went on, "But the murders don't make sense unless *Lorimer* knew about the oil." I paused. "Lorimer — or Lou Grecian." Maybe that's what had struck her as so funny. Maybe the top man hadn't been Lorimer, as I'd assumed, but Lou the Greek all along, even while he'd been in prison.

Eve was still smiling. But then she sobered and said, "Horace wanted to lease the rest of the island for an additional $40,000 and Aaron refused. He'd been paid $50,000 to guarantee his cooperation, but even after threats he refused. It was obvious his reason must have had something to do with the island. So Lou had his men go all over it and they found oil everywhere under that loose earth Aaron had covered it with — when the well came in, it must have gushed all over the place. Then Lou's men found the Christmas tree. It's in that shack out there."

"I know."

She was silent for a while. "You can't see that area from the factory, but we wondered how he managed to drill a well and bring it in without anybody else knowing about it. When we asked him, he said he worked mostly on weekends when there were only a few men at the factory, at night, and a few times when nobody else was on the island at all."

"When you asked him?" I said. "You talked to him about the oil?"

She nodded. "Horace did. Lou, too."

"Aaron admitted it?"

"Yes. We already knew about it, so there wouldn't have been any point in his denying it. Well, Horace and Lou both told Aaron he had to sell the island back. Or else."

"Or else get killed. And Aaron refused, huh?"

"No, he agreed to sell. For $4,000,000. Not just on paper like before, but in cash. Half a million in the escrow, the rest under the table. Somehow Aaron knew Horace could get that much cash, or more."

"Probably more," I said. "Handi-Foods *is* a front for distributing narcotics, isn't it?"

"I haven't the slightest idea what you're talking about."

"Back to Aaron," I said. "He *must* have known some hoodlum, probably one of Lou Grecian's gunmen, might try to knock him off." I paused. "Only he never suspected a shapely, hot-looking woman might do the job, did he?"

As if she were talking about putting the cat out. Eve said, "It never even entered his mind. Give me a cigarette."

It jarred *hell* out of me. I hadn't been able to shake the conviction that Eve was somehow trying to cross me up — perhaps by getting me to talk, tell what I knew, while not admitting anything really damaging to herself.

I lit cigarettes, handed her one. "And you shot Aaron."

"Sure, I shot him." Eve was sitting on my left, at the end of the couch; she leaned a little closer to me, looking into my face. "I shot him at about eleven-forty P.M. Saturday night. It might have been two or three minutes later, because I drove damned fast to Jim's and got there at ten of twelve." She moistened her lips, her tongue flicking. "I put my handbag on the floor by his bed. The gun was in it. When it was the right time, I just reached down in the dark and took it out. I put the gun against his side so it would muffle the noise. I'll admit I didn't think of what you said about the gun touching him. And I was . . . excited."

She stopped, her eyes slightly narrowed, staring at me.

And I started getting a very queer feeling, an odd nervousness. Something was wrong. I knew it, but I didn't know what it was. But she seemed much too, well — unafraid. Even exhilarated.

After a pause she went on, still speaking of Aaron, and this time she was even more specific than I would have wanted her to be, with blunt obscenities in her speech, a small odd smile on her lips. She told me everything, including the exact moment when she'd pulled the trigger.

I was quiet for a while. Then I said, "You didn't really know Aaron before, did you?"

"Of course not. We'd never met — that was just one of the stories Horace and I agreed to tell you. I came down from San Francisco and arranged for the job with Alexandria's so I could get next to him, even chose the name Eve so it would be easy to start a conversation about Adam and Eve. I knew if I started it, he'd do the rest. He was a pushover." Her lips curled. "Like any of you rotten men."

I heard a siren. It was faint from here, but growled to a stop below, in front of or near the hotel. She had called the police, then, after all. So we were coming to the end of it. It seemed a quiet ending for all the hell that had started there by the pool at Laguna Paradise.

I said, "I guessed I saw you making the date with Aaron near the pool Saturday night. Or was the date already made?"

She gave me a thin smile. "It was made eight days ago, Sunday, the day we met. Just like that." She snapped her fingers. "For the first night I was available. When Aaron refused to change his terms, I decided to be available Saturday night."

This gal gave me a chill. I said, "I saw you talking to Horace, too, that night. Right after Jim invited you to the party — and you said you'd have to check something first, remember? I thought fat old Horace was a customer." I shook my head. "But right then, while I actually watched, he was telling you when the police might be expected to phone Jim — in case Mickey M. failed to kill him. Telling you to go ahead, kill Aaron, and then go to Jim's — and he'd phone the police *after* midnight. Right, Eve?"

She smiled again, as she had before, as if I'd said something amusing. And when she answered the last little piece clicked into place. Because one thing, still, had puzzled me.

I knew Horace Lorimer and the gal I'd known as "Eve Angers" were man and wife, and that obviously it was not a normal marriage but a marriage of convenience. I could guess Horace might have thought it wise for the apparently honest and respectable manufacturer of Da Da Baby Foods to be a happily married — though childless — man. But for the life of me I couldn't figure out why, whether for that or other reasons, Lorimer would have chosen *Gerda* to marry.

But just before the law banged on the door, Gerda — Eve — smiling, icy contempt in her eyes, said, "You fool. He didn't tell me. I told *him*."

And then it made sense.

Twenty

Slowly, feeling a kind of warped admiration for Eve, I said, "So that's it. The top man, the brains, never was Horace, or even Lou Grecian. Horace set up the Handi-Foods front, bought the island, built his factory and all the rest of it. But he didn't dream all that up and pick you as his bride. You picked him. *You* dreamed up the operation and chose Horace as the man to front for you."

"Of course," she said simply.

And I mentally echoed: Of course. The marriage angle had bothered me as long as I'd thought it was Lorimer's idea. But from Eve's point of view it made a lot of sense. Married, Horace couldn't skip out, couldn't double-cross her, even if he'd wanted to. Legally, at least half of everything in his name — where she wanted it — was hers under California law. If he died, she would inherit it all. In case of trouble, neither under the law would be a competent witness against the other, except with the consent of both. Everything considered, it was a lovely setup — from Eve's point of view.

I said, "Then it must have been you, not your husband, who brought in Lou Grecian."

"Of course," she said again, "I knew him way back when the kids called him Greasy Louey. Even before I did my first bit in a — a correctional institution. They sent me to a school for . . ." She smiled oddly again. "For bad girls. Imagine. They said I was a bad girl, Shell."

"The hell. Why would they say a thing like that?"

She didn't have time to answer, if she was going to. The knock on the door was loud and authoritative.

And suddenly, with the first sound of that staccato rapping, Eve's face crumpled, twisted, and she burst into tears. It surprised hell out of me because it was so sudden. Her left arm lay over the arm of the divan, but she pressed her right hand over her eyes, head bent, body racked by sobs.

I guess that knock had sounded like the clang of a steel door to her. And to a gal like Eve — even a gal like Eve — the thought of growing old and lined and gray in prison was enough to turn on the tears.

I turned away from her and got up, started to step toward the door. Started to.

I don't know what warned me. I'm sure I didn't hear the sound of movement. Maybe it was the reverse — that her sobs stopped as suddenly as they had begun.

I had time to turn my head around toward her again, mildly curious, but by then she already had the bronze miniature in her hands and was straightening up. I didn't see her face. I saw the foot-high Greek god slamming through the air, the stupid baby on one side and bunch of fool grapes on the other. I even had a fractional second in which to wonder which part of the thing would clobber me — the damned baby or the damned grapes or the damned Greek. Then my head split wide open and my brain fell out. Or so, for one catastrophic moment, it seemed.

I didn't go completely out. I felt the feathery floor brush my side gently, gently, in a blend of blackness and grayness like alternating twilight and dark. And thought still functioned limply, because I heard pounding and knew it was the officers knocking at the door again only seconds after that first authoritative hammering. But I couldn't move. I didn't really much *care* to move. I heard Eve cry something in a shrill voice — then felt her hands upon me.

I thought: She's after the gun in my pocket, the little chrome-plated gun. She's going to kill hell out of me. But dizzy logic still remained somewhere in me and I thought — or felt: She can't kill me. Not now. And not while Jim may still be alive. I felt her hands tug at my shirt, my necktie. The grayness brightened and I could see her face close to mine.

Her voice was half hiss, half whisper. "If Jim is dead — or dies — I'll make it. You won't have a thing on me, *not a thing!* The only man, the *only* man, who knew I killed Aaron and shot Jim was Horace. And you killed him. Not even Lou knows about that. Aaron and Horace are dead, and if Jim dies, I'll make a chump out of you. Watch me, you bastard! Watch me!"

131

Then — incredibly — she mashed her mouth to mine, kissed me roughly, savagely, and raced toward the door.

Shock and pained astonishment made my heart pump faster, poured more strength through my body. I rolled over, got my hands beneath me and pushed against the floor. My sight cleared and I got to my hands and knees as Eve threw the door open. "Quick! Quick!" she cried.

In these past few moments she had been transformed. She was like a gal gone nuts, suddenly hysterical, wailing and shrieking, weeping — with tears on her cheeks and mascara smeared around her eyes. She had turned and was pointing at me. Beyond her, two uniformed officers, one tall and the other short and bald, stood in the doorway.

"Thank God you're here," she cried. "Arrest him! *He murdered my husband!*"

"Don't be ridiculous," I said. I still wasn't sure what Eve was trying to pull, but I knew she couldn't get away with it. I just didn't want her to get a chance to make a break. "Don't let this babe snow you guys," I went on. "She's the one you're here for — "

Eve shrieked, "Be careful, he's got a gun. Oh, thank God you're here." Then, wailing and sobbing, clenching and unclenching her hands, she said, "Oh, Horace, Horace. Darling, my darling." She sprawled by Lorimer's body, began fondling and nuzzling him.

Well, all that wailing and shrieking, fondling and nuzzling, may sound like amateur night in the little theater on Elm Street, or silent movies with sound, but it was not. It sure as hell was not. I began looking at Eve almost with warped admiration. This was real — because it wasn't just acting, a role for stage or screen; this was the big one, the life-or-death part. It was a marvelous performance.

"Over to the wall," one of the officers said to me.

"Wait a *minute*," I said, recovering my tongue. I shook my head and it felt like a piece of it fell off. But my mind was clear. At least I hoped it was. I was beginning to think I'd need it. "*She's* the one you want," I said. "She's the killer — "

"She killed her husband?"

"Oh, hell no. She killed Aaron Paradise. And shot Jim Paradise this afternoon. That's why I'm here — I'm Shell Scott. A private detective."

It didn't help that I had to tell these guys who I was. The two policemen were among those I didn't know, and obviously they didn't know me, either. They hadn't recognized me. I look like nothing in this world, but it rang no bells for them.

"Yeah?" the taller of the two officers said. "So?"

"Half the cops on the force know me, know who I am and what I am. Check with Phil Samson, Homicide Captain. He'll tell you."

"Take it easy."

Eve was still sprawled next to Lorimer, but I noted she had taken pains to sprawl on the far side of his body with her head toward us. Not only her head. She kept raising up every once in a while — in anguish I suppose — and every time she did, the excitingly low-cut neckline of the chartreuse dress got much more exciting and low cut. It looked a couple of times as if you-know-what were going to spill clear out onto Horace. The policemen also noticed.

"Over to the wall," the officer said. "To the wall."

"You sound like a Cuban Communist," I said. "To the wall, indeed — "

"*Get* over there."

They had me put my hands on the wall, feet back, while one of them shook me down. "You guys are making a very fatheaded mistake," I said.

"Just routine. We'll get your statements. That guy *is* dead over there. Just routine."

I shut up. When things simmered down a bit I could clear up everything, I knew, and there was no sense antagonizing the fatheads unduly. Eve had made a nice try, but no woman, not even a woman as shapely and sexy and clever as Eve, was going to make a monkey out of me.

They took the Colt Special from my holster, Eve's empty gun from my right coat pocket and the .32 automatic from the other. Then they let me turn around.

"Please listen to me for a moment," I said quietly. "The woman is Gerda Lorimer, also known here as Eve Angers. She's the one you want. That's why I called the complaint . . . board. . . ."

Then I got it. Late again.

The tall officer — his name was Vingger, I'd discovered — said, "Sure. Only it was a lady called in." He turned to Eve, who was now standing by Lorimer's body. "You the one phoned in, lady?"

"Yes, officer." She sobbed, her chest heaving. And when her chest heaved, that was a lot of heaving. She mashed one hand against her breasts, so hard that the creamy white flesh was pressed, bulging, over the chartreuse cloth. "This man — Mr. Scott — forced his way in here, shot my husband, then accused me of — oh, insane things." She put a hand — very gently — to the side of her head. "He hit me. He said I was a murderer, a dope fiend, even . . . sexually inadequate." She mashed her breasts again. Obviously, I was wrong about everything.

The short, bald policeman said to me, "How about it? Did you shoot him?"

"Hell, yes. But he came at me with a gun — that little chromed automatic — and tried to kill me. So I had to — "

"That's a lie!" Eve stood straighter, quivering with righteous indignation, her face twisted — but not too twisted. "He *murdered* my husband. Horace was defenseless, and he murdered him. I carry a little gun in my bag, the little automatic, and he took that. Not that I could have used it — he already had two guns of his own. Then he grabbed me and kissed me — "

My mouth dropped open. "Grabbed her and *kissed* her — "

"Kissed me and kissed me, and then he tried to . . ." She broke it off, agonized by the memory.

Vingger was looking at my mouth. And right then I got the first twinge of apprehension. Slowly I raised a hand to my chest. My tie was loosened, pulled crookedly to one side. Two buttons were gone from my shirt. And I knew there would be a smear of orange-red lipstick on my mouth.

"Now, look," I said. "Hold it a minute. This woman is the dead man's wife. His name was Horace Lorimer, and he was . . ." I stopped.

What could I tell them? That he cheated on his income tax? I didn't have any proof of narcotics smuggling — not yet. And, with a creepy sensation, I realized maybe I never would have.

Eve spoke. "My husband is — was — a baby-food manufacturer. He made Da Da Baby Food."

That didn't exactly make him sound like a fiend in human form. I said, "Maybe so. But — do you know Captain Feeney? Head of Narcotics?"

"I know who he is," Vingger said.

"Well, Lorimer was suspected of being a dealer in narcotics. Right now the Captain is in San Pedro checking a tip I gave him. He may even have the goods on Lorimer — the late Lorimer — by now."

Vingger nodded. He didn't act as if he thought I was lying; nor did he give the impression he believed me. He was noncommittal. He hadn't treated me roughly in any way, and was just getting both sides of the story, as he should have.

My head started throbbing more violently all of a sudden. I squinted, put a hand on the big lump at my hairline. The skin was cut there, laid open for about an inch. Blood was wet on my forehead.

Vingger said, "How'd that happen?"

"She clobbered me with a goddamn statue."

"Fortunately, I did manage to," Eve said. "When he was kissing . . . and all — we were on the divan there . . ." She let it trail off.

That one chilled me. A little late, I began to understand just how good Eve was. Not only had she planned everything — fast — even before phoning the police, but she was giving it just the right touch, dropping in each little bit at precisely the right moment, when it would be most convincing, have the most telling effect.

Now she went on in a rush, "We were on the divan. I — I reached back and grabbed the statuette. I hit him — " She jerked her head to one side. "Then I called the police. But a minute or so ago he started coming to. I didn't know what to do. Thank God you got here when you did."

"Oh, nuts," I said. "It won't work, Eve. I'll admit you're good. With somebody else you might make this stick — but not with me, you won't."

I turned to the police officers and said, "She had to make this up in a hurry, and she did pretty well with what she had. But I ask you, does it make sense that I'd come in here and knock off her husband, then start making goo-goo eyes at this babe? Man, there are easier ways. Me, I go for soft lights and sweet music, and corpses cool my ardor. If she says the little automatic is hers, you can bet it is. But Lorimer ran into the bedroom and got it — "

"He didn't — "

I glared at her. "Eve, shut up. Or I'll come over there and bat you one." I looked at the policemen. "Even if I get shot doing it."

She shut up.

I stood there and told the officers what had really happened, hitting it fast, just covering the high points.

Then Vingger said, "Uh-huh. Let's all go downtown."

The other officer had used the phone to call Headquarters. Now he said, "Don't touch that statchoo, please, lady."

Eve had started to pick up the lumpy gadget she'd swatted me with. She straightened up and said, "I'm sorry. I was just going to put the Hermes back on its pedestal."

I said, "The *what?*"

Suddenly the name rang a bell. Like the bell which tolls for whom. And I guess you know for whom.

Eve glanced at me. "The Hermes," she said. "Of Praxiteles."

Fine. Great. A similar statchoo had been used by that kid from Lupo's in San Francisco when he'd batted his sweetie on the noodle. If I had recognized the damn thing it might have raised my hackles a little, put me on guard — and saved me a lot of trouble.

But, of course, I hadn't recognized it. Sometimes I feel I lack culture.

Vingger said again, "Let's go downtown."

We went.

Twenty-One

The Homicide Squadroom is on the third floor of L.A.'s Police Building, and I guess I'd been up there a thousand times — under happier circumstances.

My firmest, oldest friend in Los Angeles is the Captain of Homicide, Phil Samson. Good friends, too, are Lieutenant Rawlins, Sergeant Casey, a dozen others in the Homicide Division alone. I know perhaps five hundred L.A. police officers well enough to jaw with, or cut up touches with over a cup of coffee. And most of them know the truth: that I've never lied to one of them, not once.

I've been called a nut, a lecherous s.o.b., a fool, an uncouth slob, and an uncultured idiot among even more colorful descriptions, most of them fairly accurate; but nobody who knows me has ever accused me of being a liar. Naturally Eve couldn't know that. But it was still rough.

Because Eve went all the way. She told her story again almost as well as she'd created it the first time, and she swore out a complaint against me and signed it.

I told my story, too. But when I got through there was no evidence on which Gerda Lorimer could be held. I hadn't realized it, before, but — until and unless Jim could give testimony corroborating parts of my story — there was not a damned bit of evidence against her. Horace was dead; Aaron was dead; and Jim was unconscious — or dying.

She was Horace Lorimer's wife, yes. So what? She'd been working as a model at Laguna Paradise. So what? She'd been at a party with Jim and me Saturday night; she'd called herself Eve Angers; she — and her dear departed husband — occasionally went to the Purple Room. Again, so what?

The chromed automatic was registered in the name of Gerda Lorimer, all right. The gun from Eve's bag, with which I'd shot Horace, wasn't registered to either of them; probably it was stolen. Eve claimed I'd brought it to the suite; I said it had been in her handbag. There was no proof either way. The police kept the gun so test bullets could be compared with those in Lorimer — and Jim — and Aaron.

Eve denied everything that depended on my word alone, the things I couldn't prove, that is; I denied practically everything she said. But I couldn't link her to any crime, not yet; and after all *I* had shot her husband.

So they were going to let her go. They had to.

They were going to let me go, too. Some points had to be stretched a little, but all I had actually done was shoot Lorimer in self-defense, and that's the way it was written down, "pending the outcome of investigation."

I was in the Homicide Squadroom with Captain Samson and Phil Rawlins. Sam is a big, hard guy with a well-concealed marshmallow heart, iron-gray hair and always-clean-shaven face. He wiggled his big, solid jaw as he clamped strong teeth on a black cigar and growled, "What did you expect, Shell?"

"But dammit, I *know* she's guilty."

"I've heard that song from you before — more times than I like to think about. All we've got is what you *say*. Where's your physical evidence? Where's your corroboration? We can't make Lorimer say anything — you fixed that."

"Yeah, I fix everything."

"Paradise can't talk. Not yet, anyway. And you haven't got any proof about all this Brea Island business. If Feeney comes up with some H in that damned squashed bananas or whatever it is, he'll go out there and *then* maybe you'll have something. But if he doesn't — "

"Wait a minute." Something he'd said a little while ago was sticking in my mind. Something about "physical evidence."

"Well, there she goes," Sam said.

I glanced over my shoulder. Eve had been in an interrogation room, and now she was just passing the open door outside this room. Free as a bird.

I swore under my breath, stepped into the hall and watched her walk away from me. She moved gracefully, hips swaying seductively over the long, lovely legs, as they had Saturday night when she'd walked from Jim and me near the pool. Those flaring hips, that dangerous derrière, swinging, swaying, as graceful — and as deadly — as the head of a cobra.

Talk about physical evidence, she sure had plenty of evidence to prove she was physical. She really looked like the original Eve — on the outside, anyway.

And then it clicked. I grinned.

"Eve!" I called.

I didn't run after her. But when she turned I motioned for her to come back. She hesitated, then shrugged and walked toward me. I led her into the Homicide Squad-room. Samson looked up and scowled. Rawlins grinned slightly, wondering what I was up to.

"Watch the door," I said to him. "Catch her if she runs."

Rawlins grinned. "I'll catch her."

I turned and looked at Eve. "I don't know how I missed it this long," I said. "Always just right, always in place — and those little-girl bangs. But mainly Sunday morning, remember? You were wearing a towel. You'd just gotten up, just stepped out of the shower. But your hair was perfect, not even damp, Eve. Or rather your wig was; probably your hair was a mess."

The only change was in her eyes. Then her lips thinned a little.

It wasn't easy. She didn't want me to take the damned thing off — and probably she could sue me for violating her person, or at least her head; and even Samson tried to stop me. But I thought: So sue me; so throw me in jail.

I got it off.

It was elastic in back, and had a small comb in front and several bobby pins stuck in it here and there. Her hair was a kind of orange blonde, matted and mussed and not very nicely waved, but quite attractive, nonetheless. To me, it was beautiful.

"Sam," I said, "Wes Simpson told me the lab boys took a couple of blonde hairs from Aaron's pillow — Eve, naturally, doesn't know that." I pointed to her head. "That's where they came from. And I'll bet the boys in S.I.D. can prove it."

Eve looked at me, her face flushed, eyes colder than her heart, I said, "Tell me one thing. Did you take the wig off while you were with Aaron? Or did you go there as a blonde to save wear and tear on your wig-do and show up at Jim's as a nicely-groomed black-haired sex-pot?"

She never did answer me. At least she didn't answer the question. She said to me again, slowly and venomously and distinctly, "You . . . rotten . . . bastard."

A little later, only minutes before six P.M., Samson said, "Don't get giddy, Shell. We can hold her, sure. This doesn't mean we can keep her. A couple of blonde hairs — that's not motive, means, and opportunity. And she claims she was there on Thursday night, not Saturday. Can you prove different? Prove?"

"Somehow I'll prove it."

"Well, she might not be here when you get back unless you come back with more than we've got now. She just called one of the most high-powered and influential attorneys in Los Angeles. I don't know how long we can keep her."

"Keep her as long as you can. I'll see that babe in Techachapi if it kills me."

I left in a hurry and called Ed Klein.

Fortunately, the sea was fairly calm. For twenty bucks, a kid named Smith had brought me out here, on the ocean a mile off the beach at Balboa, in his twenty-four-foot Chris Craft. After phoning Ed Klein from L.A. I'd made it to Balboa in less than an hour, but there was less than an hour's daylight left.

A little plane zoomed low overhead, wobbling about unduly, I thought. It had small oblong doodads instead of wheels, so I assumed it was the seaplane bringing Ed and his friend to pick me up. But it was sure a *little* plane. And it looked sort of loosely put together, as if several nuts and bolts were missing.

The kid said, "What's he doing, stunting?"

"You got me." The plane snorted above us about two hundred feet away, making a great clatter which reminded me of a model A with loose cylinders and no exhaust pipe. It started to turn and, strange to say, sort of skidded sideways in the air.

"I didn't know they could do that," the kid said.

"Neither did I." The plane straightened, went up in the air a bit, then began a slow, wide, sloppy turn and finally was coming back at us, very low this time.

"Didn't look like much fun, did it?" the kid said.

"Looked kind of, ah, scary, huh?"

"Yeah. Maybe it was a accident."

"Don't say that! Don't say accident." I lowered my voice. "I'm sure Ed's pilot knows what he's doing."

"Sorry. But, boy! You couldn't get me up in that old crate for a million dollars."

"Look, maybe we'd better not talk at all." I was starting to feel a mild apprehension. And I wasn't even in the plane yet. It was about fifty yards away now, maybe six feet above the water, and coming at us. Straight at us. Straight —

"What's he *doing*?" the kid said.

"Looks like he's trying to, ha-ha, scare us. But he'll just — AAAH!"

The plane wobbled about a bit, then its nose went up and it shot over us, but not very far over us. About an inch. I looked around at the kid. He wasn't in sight. Where'd he go? Then he crawled over the side of the boat. He was all wet.

After another goofy turn like a half-Immelmann, the plane was finally down on the water and taxiing toward us and I was standing at the Chris Craft's bow. In a minute the seaplane was close enough for me to leap at the open door in its side. I leaped.

I managed to climb in without drowning, stumbled toward one of two seats up front — the co-pilot's seat, I guessed — and fell into it.

Ed Klein was in the other seat, on my left. "Here we go," he said.

I looked around. "Go?" I didn't see anybody but me and Ed in the plane. "Where's the pilot?"

Vroom. We were moving, bouncing and clattering over the ocean, propeller whirring, pontoons, or whatever the damned things were, slapping the water.

"I'm the pilot!" Ed yelled, as if the thought horrified even him.

"Ye Gods! You're the pilot? You're a licensed pilot?"

"Who said anything about licensed?"

"Oh-h." I shut my eyes. We bounced what I guessed must have been a thousand feet in the air and then banged down on that hard water. Then we bounced again. We were going to die!

"I want to go to the toilet," I said. But suddenly I noticed the ride seemed smoother. I opened my eyes and we were tearing along at incredible speed a foot or two over the ocean.

"How fast are we going?" I asked casually at the top of my lungs.

"Oh, maybe a hundred miles an hour."

It was fifty times that. "Get this thing in the air, way up in the air. For crissakes," I said.

"I'll get it in a minute," Ed said. "Don't make these things like they used to."

"Like they *used* to? Great balls of fire, this is worse than a Spad without wheels. Von Richtofen probably shot this thing down in World War — Oh!" We were *way* up in the air. "Get this thing lower!" I shouted.

"Oh, hell, you aren't afraid of a little airplane, are you?"

"I couldn't feel worse if this one was shooting at me. But I'm not afraid of the airplane. What I'm afraid of is the world down there. Do you know what you're doing? Ed, do you know what you're doing? Ed! Say something!"

"I take it you don't fly much."

"Not much. And never again. I'll walk after this."

He chuckled. 'Not on the water, you won't."

"I may before this trip is over."

Ed pulled a pint of Old Crow from his pocket. It was only half full.

"You've been drinking," I said.

"Naw." The cork went *thoonk* as he pulled it out, then he put the bottle to his mouth and slugged down two or three fingers.

"You," I said, "have been drinking."

"Naw, not even a pint yet." He extended his hand. "Have some of this. It'll put hair on your chest."

"Who wants hair on his chest? Besides," I added stuffily, "I don't drink out of bottles." Then I drank out of the bottle.

Somehow we made it.

Truly, I don't remember how we got down on the water and taxied into the bay and tied up at the dock. That memory, mercifully, is buried deep, deep, in some dark horribleness of my brain. The first thing I remember is lying flat on the wooden planks of the dock. "Oh, boy," I was saying. "Oh, boy. Never again."

Ed sprang lightly to the dock carrying a suitcase filled with tools he'd brought along. "Hurt yourself?" he asked.

I got up. "No. I was just . . . relaxing."

"Well, move lively. Let's get a look at that well before it's dark."

The sun was low on the horizon when we reached the bunkhouse, but there was enough light left if we hurried. From his suitcase Ed took two crowbars and we started ripping off the end of the building. In less than five minutes we had an opening six feet high.

Ed dropped his crowbar, a happy smile on his deeply tanned face. "Yes, sir. That's a Christmas tree," he said. "You got yourself a well."

I stepped up near him as he eyed the mess of pipes and valves, then got a wheel wrench from his suitcase and started to turn a valve with it. Then he stopped and said to me, "Better move aside, Shell. You're right where the oil should come out. Not connected to a line, so we'll just let her flow a bit."

I moved aside. He freed the valve, then turned it by hand. At first it was just a trickle, then it gushed. Ed spun the valve and stepped back with a whoop, and on his face was the expression of a man looking on something he loves. "Baby, baby," he yelled, "there she goes."

Oil, thick and black, spurted from the pipe like black blood from a cut artery. It streamed from the Christmas tree and spread on the ground, running in a thick river away from us down a shallow furrow in the earth.

And a queer feeling gripped me. I knew, then, that until this moment I hadn't really believed it. I'd just sort of gone on faith to here, but now I could see it, touch it, smell it. Oil. Oil, growling up from deep in the earth, pushed by Nature's gases, and for one brief moment of brighter awareness I could see it, refined, split, joining in new chemical compounds — in cars, generators, lamps, diesels; driving engines and smoothing bearings; in hundreds of products with thousands of uses, from farming to photography, plastics, medicines . . . And there all the time for the man with faith enough and strength enough to find it and seize it.

Ed yelled, "Boy, you got a big one!" and sort of pranced about on the balls of his feet. We both ran around a little, and stopped five or ten yards out in the open, staring at the gushing stream of oil. Ed looked like a kid, dancing about and grinning, his face glowing.

"Goddamn," he yelled, "I wish I'd brought it in. I wish it was mine."

Then he stopped suddenly. He stared at me. There was an almost violent expression on his face. The thought occurred to me — a ridiculous thought, of course — that maybe Ed really *did* wish the well was his. Maybe he was willing to do violence if there was a chance he could get it. Maybe he'd snapped, flipped, gone cuckoo.

All this went through my mind in about half a second. And in the next half-second I considered the fact that I really didn't know anything about him. I'd just met him this afternoon. For all I knew — but, hell, he wouldn't really do anything violent. And if he tried, well, I still had my .38 in its shoulder holster. But all these dopey thoughts were ridiculous, naturally. I liked old Ed.

And then he yanked out a gun and shot me.

At least that is sure what he appeared to be doing.

Ed's face contorted in a kind of snarl and he yanked an enormous old blunderbuss from beneath the belt of his pants and he aimed it at my head.

"Hey!" I yelled.

I knew what had happened. The lust for oil had unhinged him. He had become an oil maniac. Black-gold fever was snarling in his veins. He was going to kill me.

The hell he was. I went into a crouch and my hand flashed with lightning speed to my shoulder holster and —

BLAM! Ed fired.

The bullet whistled past my head. He'd missed me.

Then I heard the big slug smack something behind me and heard the high, thin cry. I spun around. A man was turning in the air ten feet away, at the corner of the bunkhouse. He fell, rolled. I saw the lean length of him, the scraggly mustache. Beanpole.

Ed said, "Didn't have time to tell you to move, son. He had a bead on you and there just wasn't time."

"Ed — " But neither was there time to say what I wanted to say. We had known there was a good chance the muggs at the Handi-Food factory might spot the plane coming in and landing, but we hadn't been sure what they would do then. Now we were sure.

They'd come trotting over here and when they'd seen the oil — spreading all over the place now — had determined we couldn't be allowed to leave the island alive. Apparently the whole gang had come trotting, too, because as I yanked my head around I saw half a dozen men twenty or thirty yards away, out past the end of the bunkhouse. Only one of them had a gun in his hand but he raised it and fired at me. I yanked out my Colt and snapped a shot at him as Ed yelled, "Over here! There's some guys on this side."

The hell with over there. I didn't even have time to look. I missed the man I'd shot at but he was firing again and the others were hauling out guns. I just blazed away, knocking one man down and bitting another — apparently in the leg. His leg jerked and he fell, but got up and ran. The others ran out of sight too, racing toward the opposite end of the bunkhouse from where Ed and I were.

So, finally, nobody was shooting at me. But my gun was empty. I'd heard Ed's big revolver blamming two or three times, and as I turned toward him a gun cracked and the sleeve of Ed's shirt jumped. A small red stain appeared on the white cloth. He spun, agile as a cat, dropped to one knee bringing his gun up. Then he leaped behind the bunkhouse wall, near the Christmas tree.

"Can't see where it came from," he yelled. "Get in here, boy. They'll kill you out there."

But I wasn't going in there, not yet. When Beanpole fell I'd seen his gun drop to the ground, flipping four or five yards past the building's wall. And I wanted that gun. I didn't know what was out of sight around the wall there where the guy had been. But I'd know in a minute.

I turned, spotted the gun, bent low and ran toward it. I scooped it up, grabbed it tight in my hand and left my feet, rolling. I could feel the bandaged wound high near my neck tear open, and my head started aching enormously, but I came up on my knees with the gun cocked and in my right fist.

A big burly man jumped out of sight around the far end of the building. Lou the Greek. But halfway between him and me stood another man. As I spotted him he fired. He missed. I didn't. I snapped off one shot and he slammed back against the boards behind him, then went straight down and stayed propped against the building, his head lolling forward and to one side, chin on his chest. The gun was a Colt .45, a heavy automatic pistol; he wouldn't move again.

Then it was quiet. Except for the massive whisper of oil gushing from the pipe. It was flowing even more rapidly now than before, spreading in a great pool around us. It was under my feet, slick, smoothly moving around and over my shoes.

I jumped back toward the little room where Ed was, Ed and the Christmas tree. Movement on my left flickered in the corner of my eye. Ten yards away, crouched behind one of the low gray shrubs, a man moved. The last rays of sunlight bounced from the gun in his hand.

The gun was leveled, steady — aimed at Ed Klein. I flipped the automatic toward him and fired three times as fast as I could squeeze the trigger. I couldn't afford to waste any of the few bullets we had. But I couldn't afford to waste Ed, either. One of the slugs, or more, hit the man. He whirled, as if someone had yanked him around hard, and went down on his face.

I ran toward Ed, slipped in the oil and fell, got up and made it into the room we'd ripped open.

Ed's face was grim, but he wasn't pale or panicky. "The sonsofbitches," he said. "They never even seen me before."

"Doesn't make any difference. They'd kill anybody who found this well, Ed, as long as they thought they could get away with it. And unless we can make it to the plane, they'll get away with it."

There was a lull in the action. I figured nobody would try to pick us off or rush us for another minute or two — not with at least three of their men already dead or dying out there. But there wasn't a chance we could hold off all these guys for long. As soon as our ammunition was gone —

"How many shells do you have left in that cannon?" I asked Ed.

"Two."

I checked the automatic's clip, shoved it back into place and cocked the gun again. "I've got three."

"Five, altogether. Even if you shoot as good as I do, we can't hit more than five of 'em. And I'd guess there's more than five."

"Yeah. And simple addition subtracts us. Maybe we'd better make a break for it now."

"Either that," Ed said, "or try to hang on for another five, ten minutes. It'll be dark enough by then so we'd have a better chance."

The sun had just set and it was dusk, the gray time before full darkness, but with enough glow still in the air so that we could see anything that moved near us. And vice versa. Three shots rang out then two more. Splinters flew from the remaining walls around us.

"Take it back," Ed said. "Guess they don't have to see us to hit us. We better — " He stopped, raised his head. "Listen."

I could hear the crackling sound, like someone walking on eggshells. I noticed the blackened earth around us seemed to be pulsing, getting brighter and then darker.

It hit us both at the same time.

"The sonsofbitches are burning us out," Ed said.

It was true. The far end of the bunkhouse was on fire. We could hear the crackling sound easily now, building up to a roar. Through thin cracks in the wall behind us we could see the redness of flame inside the bunkhouse itself.

"Way this place caught so fast," Ed said, "they must've used gasoline to start — keerist!"

"What's the matter?"

"The damn fools! Shell, if you never saw an oil well afire, you're going to see something you'll never forget as long as you live."

"I should remember it a good two or three minutes." Only then did it penetrate. Those idiots had set fire to the bunkhouse, and in minutes — or seconds — the *oil* would be aflame, the well burning. *And we were standing on top of the well.*

"Ed," I yelled. "Turn it off, turn the thing off!"

"You want us to stay here and get fried?" Ed said. "Let's go!"

Ed was a man who made up his mind in a hurry. He just started running like a wild rabbit toward the dock and our plane even before the last word was out of his mouth, the word getting fainter as he ran. Just "Let's — " and then he was moving — "GOOOOOoooo-ooo-o."

For the first few yards he would have the element of surprise, I figured, and I intended to give him a little — very little — head start and then go after him. Besides which, he had left me here flatfooted. But he'd taken no more than a dozen steps when he stopped suddenly, his feet slipped in the oil, and he fell.

I jumped forward, but before I could reach him he was on his feet and coming back toward me. "What the hell?" I said. "Want me to go first?"

"We ain't going." He pointed.

I followed the line of his arm toward the dock where we'd tied up. In the gathering gloom I could see a flickering red glow.

"Looks like something's burning there, too," I said. "There where we — the *plane!*"

Before the word was out of my mouth the plane's gas tanks went. A small puff of red bloomed and seemed to lift itself in the air then settle back toward the sea. A couple of seconds later the boom of the explosion reached us.

We were in the open now, exposed, and three or four shots rang out. None of them was close, but, although it was nearly dark, light from the fire illumined the area clearly. The whole bunkhouse was going now, flames leaping scarlet against the sky, smoke and swirling red sparks shooting up in the air.

Ed and I both spoke at the same time. "Here they come," I said, and he yelled, "Hey, there's a boat!"

Seven or eight men — not in a bunch, but coming from different directions — were running toward us, bent low toward the ground.

I fired twice at the nearest men and one of them fell heavily. The other one dived to the ground. Ed's gun blasted and I saw a man spin, straighten up, stand erect for a long second and fall. I'd counted the three shots; two slugs left, one apiece.

The running men had stopped running and flopped to the ground, but they had been — and still were — firing at us. I didn't think either of us had been hit, but there was pain in my left arm now, and on one thigh a red stain mingled with the oil that smeared me, smeared both Ed and me.

We flopped flat on the ground, side by side. Ed was swearing softly. I said to him, "What was that about a boat?"

He pointed. Very near the shore a boat was turning. I could see the green starboard light swinging as the boat turned to its port.

"What in hell is it?" Ed yelled. "The goddamn Mafia?"

"Beats me." I squinted. It was a big sonofagun, painted white, maybe a hundred feet long. Aft of the wheelhouse, amidships, was a big gun, some kind of cannon. In the air above it, at the top of the mast, a flag or pennant fluttered. Another ensign flew from the stern.

A searchlight came on, swept over us. And as the boat continued turning I saw the big black figures on the bow: CG-95375.

It was a Coast Guard boat, one of the 95-foot patrol boats.

The ensign atop the mast was the Coast Guard Ensign; that cannon I'd seen was a 20-millimeter gun; and the flag rippling at the stern was the American flag.

"Ed," I shouted. "That's a Coast Guard boat!"

"Ye Gods! Are we at war with them, too?"

Again I said, "Beats me."

What in hell *was* a Coast Guard boat doing here? Either Brea Island was being invaded, or —

Then I remembered: Feeney. Maybe. Maybe . . . If he'd found that marked case of spinach, and *if* that can of bananas . . .

I didn't complete the thought.

WHOOOOM! It was a huge but almost velvety sound. A red glare seemed to envelop the whole island. Air fluttered against my eardrums.

"There she goes," Ed said, and his voice was soft.

The oil was burning. Black smoke boiled upward above where the bunkhouse had been. But I could see the Christmas tree clearly, the black gush of oil and then fire — and more. It looked as if the earth was burning, as if this area of the island was aflame. And the flames came toward us. The oil, spilled here on the earth, was burning. And we were lying — covered with the thick black fluid — flat on the oil-sodden earth.

Ed was on his feet first. And again I heard him say, "Let's GOOOOOoooo-ooo-o."

As I jumped up I saw the fire sweep over a man who had been lying close to the bunkhouse — lying in a pool of oil that was suddenly a pool of flame. He leaped to his feet. But even before that he had started screaming. He ran, his oil-soaked clothing in flames, the sound of his hoarse, harsh, agonized scream one of the most bone-chilling sounds I'd ever heard.

I was standing erect, and the flames were coming closer to me, the wave of heat searing my face, but I couldn't take my eyes off the man. He ran for ten, perhaps twelve steps and then fell. For another second or two he screamed, more faintly, then the sound stopped.

I heard the siren again. I turned to run after Ed. Then — behind me there was a horrible sound, like three or four dinosaurs burping. I turned around.

My mouth dropped open.

And I said stupidly, "What happened?"

Twenty-Two

It was a Saturday in June again, a week after the whole thing had started. Only a week, with the ugly memories still fresh. Even so, I felt very good indeed. For several reasons.

For one, Jim had come through the operation in good shape the previous Monday afternoon and was resting comfortably now, getting stronger, and in a few minutes I could visit him for the first time. For another, I had a date tonight with — who else? With Laurie Lee.

Eve was in the can awaiting trial — late Monday night Jim was able to tell the police she'd shot him — as were Lou Grecian and eleven of his "employees" who had still been alive when a whole boatload of men, including Captain Feeney, arrived at Brea Island. That's who it had been, all right, in the Coast Guard patrol boat. Captain Feeney had been along, but primarily as an observer; the men who came pouring ashore were U.S. Customs Agents along with agents of the Federal Bureau of Narcotics.

It had taken Feeney and his men a little time to locate the spinach case which contained the can I'd switched, but when it was opened they found in it seven ounces of mashed bananas and one ounce of uncut heroin. Feeney had notified the Federal Bureau of Narcotics, and from then on the L.A.P.D. stepped aside while federal agents took over. They'd piled into a Coast Guard boat and headed for the known source of the narcotics, Brea Island — and those two cases of "mashed bananas" which were still on the factory floor. Two cases, ninety-six cans — minus the one I'd lifted. Ninety-five cans, then, each containing an ounce of heroin. Ninety-five ounces, or nearly six pounds, approximately two and three-quarter kilos of pure, unadulterated heroin. And a hell of a lot of mashed bananas.

The rest was anticlimactic, but one of the high spots of the night was the fact that Ed Klein and I got to return to the mainland — on a boat. No more planes for me.

I parked the Cad in the lot of Drayton Memorial Hospital where Jim had been transferred from the Loma Drive Receiving Hospital, and walked through bright sunshine to the entrance. At two o'clock on the nose I walked through the door of Jim's private room.

He was propped up in bed, not quite so deeply tanned as before, but clean-shaven, grinning at a redheaded nurse. "Oh, Jimmy," she was saying as I stepped inside, "you're *awful*."

He spotted me and waved. The nurse turned and started out, blushing. I said, "He's better, huh?"

"Better?" she said. "He's worse!"

The door closed behind her as I grabbed Jim's outstretched hand and shook it. His grip was firm, and his blue-green eyes were bright.

"Imagine," he said, "hard-boiled Shell Scott sending flowers."

I had sent him a bedpan planted with sweet peas. "Better than a wreath," I said. "You look pretty good, Jim."

"Be out in another week, they tell me." He shook his head. "I'm alive, but scarred to hell and gone. Bullets, scissors, scalpels, stitches. It will ruin me for strip poker." He scowled. "Which is probably a damned good thing."

Jim knew only part of what had happened, and that had come at him in bits and pieces, so I went over most of it from the beginning, then said, "Incidentally, Jim, I think I know what was in your mind when you tried to tell me who'd plugged you. But I'd like to hear it from you."

"Sure. Well, I opened the door — carefully, hand on the gun in my pocket — and saw Eve. Naturally, I wasn't worried about her."

"Naturally not."

"I gave her a smile, asked what she wanted. All of a sudden a gun was in her hand and she said, 'I'm not Eve, Jim. There isn't anybody named Eve — I'm Horace Lorimer's wife. And I'm going to kill you. I killed your brother.' She even told me how it was, the way she — " He cut it off.

I said, "I can imagine. In fact, I know."

"Well, she told all that, smiling like an angel. I just stood there. I couldn't believe it at first. But, finally I tried to get out my gun, and *wham!* She shot me. I passed out, but came to once, before you showed up. I couldn't move, but I could think and I realized even if I got a chance to tell somebody who'd shot me I didn't know her name. The gal I knew as Eve Angers was undoubtedly going to suddenly disappear, maybe within the hour — and I didn't even know how long I'd been passed out."

"She'd already disappeared by the time I talked to you, Jim. In a way. She'd checked out of the Claymore, and later met hubby at a bar. And she was scheduled for a seven P.M. flight to San Francisco." I grinned. "Which she missed."

"It figures. Well, then you asked me for the *man's* name." He grinned back at me. "That shook me a little. If I told you it was Eve — and Eve had vanished — she'd get away with it. You wouldn't even know where to start looking. But I knew you could find Lorimer — and Lorimer's wife. Once you saw her you'd know the whole thing." He wagged his head. "What I tried to tell you was 'It was Lorimer's wife — Eve, but Eve's not her name.' Something like that. I just couldn't quite make it."

"I should have been able to figure it out anyway, I guess. But I didn't until I actually found Lorimer and Eve together, and realized they were married."

Jim mashed out his cigarette, a slight frown on his face. "Look, Aaron was killed because of the oil on Brea Island. They were after the oil, right?"

"That's right."

"Well, I would inherit from Aaron. I can understand they couldn't buy the island from me and then start drilling more wells, bringing in oil, because that would for sure have told me why he was killed. But what good would it do them to kill *both* of us?"

"You told me yourself that day on your boat, coming back from the island, Jim. With both of you dead, the estate would escheat — that is, would go to the state. The executor might dispose of the estate in order to settle the claims of the U.S. and then California governments, and the Lorimers and Lou felt sure they could easily arrange to buy the island, either through pulling strings — of which they could pull plenty — or, if it was sold at auction, putting in a very fat bid. Handi-Foods Inc., of course, had the perfect justification for bidding big on the land. Even if that didn't work, they were prepared to forge an option to purchase — an option which would have survived the death of the owner and prevail against anybody else's claim. Or so Ralph Merle tells me. Besides, ignoring the financial angle, they couldn't afford to have anybody else setting up shop on the island, for oil or any other reason — not with the narcotics factory they had going next door."

He nodded slowly. "What people won't do for money. Of course" — he smiled — "it's a *lot* of money. Incidentally, you told me about all the excitement out there and then Feeney arriving, but you never finished, pal. How much oil does it appear *is* out there?" He grinned. "On my island."

"None. There isn't any oil."

I thought he was going to go into shock, have a relapse, or a stroke, or maybe even get out of bed. But finally he simmered down and was quiet for a long time.

Then he said, "The sonofabitch."

"Yeah. That well was the old oil, all right, Jim. The joker in the deck. And Aaron stacked the deck. He was an oilman for a while, sure. But more than anything else, he was a con man. And that's what the well, the dirt-covered oil all over the ground, the greasy bunkhouse, the whole works was: a big, fat confidence game. In the old days men salted mines with hunks of gold then sold the 'gold mine' to the suckers. Aaron simply salted — or oiled — an oil well. A well which, of course, he never actually drilled. What he was after was four million bucks from a gang of crooks. What he got was a bullet."

Jim sighed. "Maybe he wasn't much good at anything else. But he was one hell of a confidence man." He shook his head. "And he sure fooled me."

"You're not alone, Jim. I fell for the con myself." I paused. "But the guy he really stuck was Lorimer. He sure did a job on him. Horace could have settled with the tax boys because he had a couple million in cash socked away, but the money was illegal profit from the sale of heroin, and he could hardly report *that* as income. Aaron showed him the way out, and all he asked for himself was fifty G's."

I lit another cigarette, dragged on it. "That fifty G's was the frosting on the cake, to make the con look good. Man, it looked so good I'm surprised Lorimer didn't go semi-legitimate. What Aaron was after, of course — and what he got — was legal, unshakeable title to Brea

Island. He leased half the island to Lorimer, the lease *not* including mineral rights. Not including, in a word: oil. Obviously, he'd dreamed up the whole caper even before he talked to Lorimer last summer. You might as well face it once and for all, Jim. Aaron never did intend to go straight, not for a minute."

"He sure suckered me," Jim said. "My own brother."

"Well, Cain clobbered Abel a long time ago. It happens."

He was quiet again for a while, then said, "How in hell did he work it? And, by the way, how did you find out? You said oil was squirting all over the place and everything was burning like crazy — what happened?"

"Well, Ed was on his way toward Catalina or somewhere, and I was about to follow him. Then there was this horrible glop, slup, burp sound and I turned and looked. I was looking right at the Christmas tree and the oil just went down to a little trickle — and stopped. I thought: Man, that is the dinkiest oil well I ever did hear of."

"I still don't quite get it. Was it running from a tank on the roof or something?"

"No, when Aaron pulled a con he did it right. We checked it the next day. He'd bought a big old steam boiler and hauled it over to the island. Dug a hole in the ground and put the boiler is it, then through a hole cut in the boiler's top dropped a length of well casing down almost to the bottom of the boiler and welded it in place. He poured in about a hundred barrels of oil, attached his Christmas tree to the casing and, through a separate valve on the boiler, crammed the air space over the oil in the boiler with air under plenty of pressure. Closed off the valve where he'd pumped in the air, covered the whole thing up with dirt, and he had a well."

"So when you opened the valve, air pressure pushed down on the oil, forced it up the pipe and out the Christmas tree."

"Yep. Hell, we *still* wouldn't know it was a con if we hadn't been so busy we didn't have time to turn off the faucet. Even Ed was nipping over the dandy well."

"Aaron sure went to a lot of trouble."

"Not trouble — not to a confidence man — but planning. Like hiding the Christmas tree, and oil on the ground — but not hiding it *too* well. Planning and effort. It cost him maybe ten, fifteen thousand dollars for the whole shebang. He was gambling for four million, after all."

After a while Jim said, "In a way, Shell, I'm glad there isn't any oil. I'll build on that island one of these days — it's mine now, legally mine. And I'll build Paradise Island yet." He sighed. "To hell with oil." I grinned at him. "As a substitute, when you get out of here, we'll get oiled together. O.K.?"

"Be my guest."

It was almost midnight again, but a very different midnight from the one a week ago. The only similarity was that Laurie was with me. That was the same. Everything else was different. And my apartment was simply stinking with smoke.

Laurie and I had hit some of the bars on the Strip, toured La Cienega, had a ball. But we hadn't eaten. No, I'd had plans. Hours in advance I had prepared everything — the chafing dishes and little alcohol doohickeys to bum under them, the cheese and french bread, steak, the works.

And suitably, mildly inebriated, I had said slyly to Laurie, "Sweets, how about a late supper in my apartment?"

And she had said gaily, "Why not?"

It had started out marvelously. I turned the lights low and lit the alcohol doohickey, and the blue flames cast a very exciting light over everything. Up to that point it was grand. Then I started cooking. I should have known, I guess, the way my mush comes out.

Stated simply, the cheese burned, the meat burned, and I burned. I couldn't even get the goddamned brandy to light in the glass. Finally I picked up a chafing dish and threw it clear the hell into the kitchenette. "O.K.," I said. "O.K."

Laurie laughed, not at all disturbed, apparently. "O.K. what?" she said.

"O.K. That's all." I glowered. "The hell with fire, anyway. I damn near got burned to a crisp on that damned island — pardon my profanity, dammit — and now, arrgh. I mean, O.K., we'll eat out. But if you order any stupid flaming — "

"Oh, Shell, relax." She was sitting on my chocolate-brown divan, leaning back against the cushions, smiling delightfully. "I'm not hungry, anyway. Come here and relax."

"I can't relax," I said.

She patted the cushions beside her. "Come on, Shell. Here, by me." She moved a little deeper into the cushions behind her.

155

"Well . . . maybe I can," I said.

I found that I could, after all.

And when I did relax I became aware of something I had never really forgotten: That this Laurie of the honey-brown eyes and devil-red lips, of the astonishing body and velvet sweetness, was something very special indeed.

And that, when it came to fire, there was no need for alcohol doohickeys when Laurie was near.

And that I was an absolute nut even to be thinking of burnt cheese and unlighted brandy at a time like this.

And that, come to think of it, I wasn't hungry, either. . . .

And a little later Laurie sighed and said sweetly, "After all, who wants a man who can *cook?*"

Biography

Richard S. Prather

Richard Prather is the author of the world famous Shell Scott detective series, which has over 40,000,000 copies in print in the U.S. and many millions more in hundreds of foreign-language editions. In 1986 he was awarded the Private Eye Writers of America's Life Achievement Award for his contributions to the detective genre. He and his wife, Tina, live among the beautiful Red Rocks of Sedona, Arizona. He enjoys organic gardening, gin on the rocks, and golf. He collects books on several different life-enriching subjects and occasionally re-reads his own books with huge enjoyment, especially STRIP FOR MURDER.

Printed in the United States
799200001B